SLY

Jagged Edge Series #4

A.L. Long

Sly: Jagged Edge Series #4

Interior edited by H. Elaine Roughton
Cover design by Laura Sanches
ASIN: B01MRT08GY
ISBN: 978-1540793393

This book is intended for mature adults only

A.L. Long

Acknowledgment

To my husband of many wonderful years, who has been so supportive of my writing. If it weren't for him my dream of writing would have never been fulfilled. I love you, sweetheart. And to my family, whom I also love dearly. Through their love and support, I can continue my passion for writing.

To the many readers, who took a chance on me and purchased my books. I hope that I can continue to fill your hearts with the passion I have grown to love.

A special thanks to all of the people that supported me at SPS. If you would like to learn about what they can offer you to become a self-publisher, please check out the link below. You will be thankful you did.
https://xe172.isrefer.com/go/curcust/allongbooks

Table of Contents

CHAPTER ONE

Nikki

As the plane accelerated down the runway, I knew it wasn't going to be long before I would be back in New York facing what was waiting for me. I wished I could change the way I was brought up, or rather, who my father was. His choices had trickled down to me in so many ways. A child should never have to pay for her parents' mistakes. Since the age of thirteen, I had been doing just that. One day I would wash my hands of him and be able to live the life every woman dreams of.

Absorbed in my own thoughts, I heard the announcement from the pilot come over the intercom. "Welcome aboard, ladies and gentlemen. Our flight will take approximately thirteen hours and forty minutes. The weather is clear and should remain so. I hope you enjoy the flight."

Looking out the window, the island that I was going to miss slowly became smaller and smaller. I hated having to say good-bye to my best friend, but I knew that Isabelle would be happy. She had been through so much over the past weeks. Just like me, her life was less than perfect. When she told me she needed to leave New York, I let her know about a job in Stillwater, OK. Who would have thought that she was a princess from Kierabali. As much as I was going to miss her, at least she would be with the man that she truly loved.

Thinking about Sly, I wondered how hard it would be on him and the other guys at Jagged Edge Security without Hawk. Hawk was a big part of the security company and would be greatly missed. They were definitely brothers, and it was evident by the way they stood beside each other during the wedding ceremony. Peter was Hawk's best man, just as I was Isabelle's maid of honor. In order for all the guys to be a part of the wedding, the bridesmaids had to be escorted up the aisle by two men instead of the traditional one-man escort. It was so hard for Hawk to decide who his groomsmen would be, until Isabelle came up with the solution to double up. Cop Coppoletti and Ash Jacobs walked Sabrina Coppoletti, Peter Hewitt and Ryan Hyatt walked Lilly Hewitt, and I was escorted by Sly Capelli and Josh Hyatt. Hawk waited for Isabelle at the altar until Mike Chavez and Lou Gainer handed her over to him. Even though it was nine men to four women, it worked out really well.

Once the captain gave the go-ahead, I reclined my seat back and tried to get some rest. I knew it was going to be a long flight, so I tried to get as comfortable as possible in the small seat. Just as I closed my eyes, I heard Sly say, "If you would like, you can use my shoulder as a pillow if it will make you more comfortable."

"Thanks," I replied, lowering my head to his broad shoulder as he lifted the armrest that separated our two seats.

This was a lot more comfortable. It felt nice to rest my head on a man's shoulder, especially Sly's. Over the past couple of weeks, we got to know each other pretty well. Even though I swore I would never get involved with an Italian man, there was something different about him. He was really sweet, and the way he looked at me with his teddy bear eyes, well, let's just say, my heart melted.

Closing my eyes, I felt him shift his body so that his arm was now wrapped around my shoulder, allowing me to nuzzle my head against his strong chest. For a man built like a brick wall, it was actually very nice using him as a pillow. Listening to his heartbeat, it didn't take long before I was asleep.

~****~

I don't remember waking up once during the flight. I must have really been exhausted. My mouth was dry except for the saliva that dribbled from the side of my mouth. Lifting my head, I looked at Sly's shirt to see that I drooled on him. I had left a big wet spot on his white t-shirt. I had never felt so embarrassed in my life.

"Hey, sunshine. Did you have a nice siesta?" Sly asked softly.

"I must have. My mouth is dry and your shirt is wet," I replied.

Peering down at his shirt where I had slobbered on him, he looked back over to me with a smile. "It's okay, sunshine. It must have been some dream you were having, the way you were mumbling in your sleep."

"Oh, God, what did I say?" I asked nervously.

"Not sure. Most of it, I couldn't understand. It was like you were telling someone to basically fuck off. You did mention the name Rosa," Sly paused. "Who is she?"

"My mother," I choked. "I need to go to the restroom."

As Sly unbuckled his seatbelt and rose to his feet, I quickly made my way down the aisle to the lavatory. The only one that was unoccupied was at the front of the plane. Making my way there, I kept wondering how much more of my dream Sly actually heard. There wasn't a day that went by that I didn't dream of my mom. Every time I closed my eyes she was there, waiting for me. Like she wanted me to join her.

My thoughts were interrupted when an elderly lady got out of her seat in front of me, heading to the lavatory. I was just about ready to tell her she needed to wait, but the way she was crossing her legs and squirming, she needed the restroom more than I did. A gentleman walked out of the lavatory and the elderly woman stepped in, turning the handle so that the 'occupied' sign was showing on the door. Even though I was the next person in line, the flight attendant must not have wanted me standing in the aisle, because he gestured for me to sit in the empty seat just outside the lavatory.

Locking myself inside, I looked at myself in the small mirror. I could see that I did more than just dream about my mom. I must have been crying at some point, because my eyes were red and surrounded by my black mascara that was supposed to be waterproof. Splashing some cold water on my face, I pulled a paper towel from the dispenser and tried the best I could to wipe some of the mascara away from my eyes. Satisfied that I looked somewhat presentable, I opened the door and headed back to my seat. I didn't think I was in the bathroom that long, but based on the number of people waiting to use the lavatory, it must have been long enough.

Taking my place, I gazed out the small window to see if there was a hint of land in sight. The only thing I could see were white fluffy clouds. Looking over to Sly, I asked with a half smile, "Do you know when we will be landing in New York?"

"A couple of hours at most," he said.

"So, any ideas on what we can do for two hours?" I asked.

"A couple, but that would mean you would need to undress," he replied with a smirk.

"Not in this lifetime, tiger."

Sly was knock-out gorgeous. He had a very muscular build, a very trusting face, and the dreamiest brown eyes I had ever seen. There were times that I caught myself looking at him wondering what kind of woman would be his type. If I would have to guess I would say he would be the type of man that liked his woman to be curvy, big breasted, with dark hair, and who could wear red lipstick so he could watch her mouth as it went down on him. Unfortunately, I wasn't any of those things. I had a nice body from years of working out in the gym. Curves, maybe a few. Big breasts, maybe, but everyone knows 'more than a handful is a waste,' at least that is what I've heard.

Bored to death, I pulled out the SkyMall magazine from the pocket behind the seat in front of me and I began looking at all the nifty things they sold. The ideas behind the products were amazing. Everything from a bike workstation to an automatic screen door. Why would anyone want to work on a laptop while riding a stationary bike? It made me wonder how much stuff was actually bought from this catalog.

Placing the catalog back in the pouch, I tilted my head back and took in a sigh of boredom. Sly must have noticed my state of mind, because he turned his body slightly my way before grabbing my hand.

"You know, Italians are known for their ability to read someone's future by looking at the palm of their hand," he declared.

"Really?" I questioned him, not believing him for a second.

Grabbing my hand, he turned it over and began concentrating on the lines on my palm. I knew that most palm readers were gypsies and they were mostly from Russia and Greece. The only Italians who claimed to be palm readers, that I knew of, were swindlers and pickpockets. Giving Sly the benefit of the doubt, I went ahead and let him do his thing.

"I can see that you have worked very hard, Based on the calluses on your hand, I would guess a gardener," he claimed. "These few cuts here may have been caused from clenching your hands, which would have caused your nails to dig into the skin."

Pulling my hand away from him, I objected, "You're crazy and way off. I haven't ever worked in a garden."

"I bet you've never boxed before either," he replied.

"Nope, wrong again."

Taking my hand again, he flipped it over and resumed where he left off. "Okay, I may have had the

15

gardener and the boxer thing wrong, but your hand does show that you use it a lot," Sly pointed out as he continued his reading. "So this line here says that you will live a long life, although this break tells me that you will have an obstacle to tackle. One so intense that it could cost you your life. It might have already happened. Were you ever close to death, Nikki?"

"Don't be silly. I am just a barista at a coffee shop. Nothing exciting there. Unless I burn to death from the steam off of the espresso machine," I replied.

When Sly was finally done reading my palm, I began to worry how close he came in knowing things about me by just looking at my hand. There were a lot of risks doing what I did during my nights. I could even get killed. So to say that I would have an obstacle to tackle was an understatement. One of the reasons I left New York to see Isabelle in Stillwater, OK was to get away from what was going to happen in New York. I knew I probably shouldn't have run, but I figured if I wasn't around, then I couldn't be forced into a situation that I knew I couldn't win.

CHAPTER TWO

Sly

I wasn't sure what was going on with Nikki, but the minute I took her hand, I knew there was more about her that she wasn't sharing. I was all too familiar with the way her hands were callused over. Even her knuckles were slightly swollen. There was only one reason they would be this way. These were defensive scars from years of fighting.

I could tell that she was uncomfortable talking about what was really going on with her. When the landing gear came down and the wheels touched down on the concrete runway, Nikki jolted off her seat like she had a fire underneath her. It was only after I saw the look on her face that I realize the jolt of the plane landing must have startled her. Placing my hand over hers, I asked with

17

concern, "Are you okay? You came off your seat like someone lit it on fire."

"I'm fine. Just don't care much for flying," she replied, taking in a deep breath.

Seeing her reaction told me it was a lot more than not liking to fly. Something else was making her jumpy. The minute the plane came to a complete stop, she couldn't get out of her seat fast enough. It was customary to let the people sitting in the front seats get off the plane first, but this wasn't the case with Nikki, The minute the seatbelt light went off, she was up and on her way to the front of the plane. She exited in such a hurry that she didn't grab the small bag she stowed in the overhead compartment when we boarded the plane.

Taking my small bag along with hers, I took my place behind the line of passengers waiting for their turn to exit the plane. I knew that Nikki was already long gone. I had no idea where she would go. Pulling out my cell, I contacted Peter to see if he still had information on her.

"Hey, bro, it's Sly," I said.

"Hey, shouldn't you be landing soon?" Peter questioned.

"Just touched down. Do you still have the information on Nikki? I need to know what her address is."

"Yeah, hold on," he answered.

As I waited for him to find the information, I kept wondering what had Nikki so riled that she had to get off the plane so fast. I've never seen a woman move so fast. Finally off the plane and in the gate area, I headed to baggage claim. My only hope was that she would be waiting at the carousel for her luggage and wouldn't forget that too.

It was no surprise that I didn't see her anywhere when I finally reached the baggage area. Nobody leaves the airport without grabbing their belongings. Something was definitely up with her. Grabbing my bag along with Nikki's pink one, I prayed that no one would be questioning why a man of my build would be toting around a pink suitcase.

More embarrassed than anything, I managed to get outside to the transportation area with only a few strange looks. Just as I entered the cab, I could hear Peter getting back on the phone.

"Jesus, dude, what did you have to do, go across town to get the information?" I cursed.

"Yeah, kind of. All the information was left at the shop. I had to make a quick trip," Peter confessed.

"You could have told me instead of keeping me on the line."

"Yeah, yeah. Do you want the information or not?"

"Give it to me," I said, closing the door to the cab.

As soon as I got the information from Peter, I instructed the cab driver to head to Brownsville. When

Peter explained to me where Nikki lived, it didn't surprise me that her hands looked the way they did. Brownsville wasn't exactly the best part of Brooklyn to live in. Pretty sure it was the crime capital of the world. With the way Nikki looked, it surprised me even more that she would be living in such a shit part of Brooklyn. *"What the hell would a beautiful girl like her be doing in Brownsville?"*

The cab driver pulled up to an old run-down apartment building. It wasn't too hard to find where Nikki lived, based on the description Peter got from Lilly and Sabrina. It was the only apartment that had bars on the windows. It was kind of funny, knowing that there was no way anyone would be able to get to her apartment from this side of the building, unless of course they carried around a forty-foot ladder. Heading inside the rundown building, I took the steps up to the third floor. It would have been a lot easier taking the elevator, only there was a big sign taped to the doors that read 'OUT OF ORDER' in big bold letters.

Lugging her pink suitcase and small bag up the flight of stairs was no easy task. I wasn't sure what she had inside, but I knew that whatever it was exceeded the forty-pound weight limit set by the airline. She must have paid an extra fifty bucks just to get this thing home. The higher I got up the steps, the louder the screaming and yelling got. I wasn't sure where it was coming from, but it was definitely between a man and a woman. There were faint cries coming from a child in the background as well. How anyone would be able to live with that yelling going on was beyond me.

Getting to her apartment, I began knocking on the door. With no answer on the other side, my only option was to take her suitcase with me to my place. Pulling out a business card from my wallet, I slipped it under her door and hoped that she was smart enough to give me a call. I didn't have anything to write with, and asking the man and woman who were yelling at each other from who knows where wasn't an option I wanted to exercise.

~****~

With thirty dollars less in my wallet, I was finally in the comfort of my own home. Placing Nikki's suitcase against the wall along with her bag, I wheeled mine to my bedroom. I was ready to relax and unwind. There was no way I was going to tackle unpacking until I had a brew. Heading to the kitchen, I opened the fridge to see that it was bare. I don't mean in the sense that there wasn't any food. There wasn't one bottle of beer inside. "Just fucking wonderful," I spat as I slammed the fridge door.

"If I would have known you would be back so soon, I would have restocked it for you," a voice said in the darkness.

Flipping the switch on in the kitchen, I saw the frame of a man staring out the window. Even though I couldn't see his face, I knew exactly who it was.

"What are you doing here, and how the fuck did you get inside my condo?" I asked, loathing the man I knew so well.

"You should know me better than that, Sylvester. I have many talents, as you know."

"What do you want, Gus?" I barked.

"Can't a father want to see how his son is doing without wanting anything?" my father asked.

"You lost that right the day you chose to work for Angelo Conti," I hissed.

I watched my father walk toward me and into the light. Even though I hadn't seen him in fifteen years, he hadn't changed very much. He was still the muscular man I knew as a child. The only difference was that his once-dark hair was now showing his age. The hair at his temples was gray and his face was lined with years of watching his back and worrying whether or not he was going to live another day.

Pulling his money clip from his front pocket, he pulled out a hundred-dollar bill and placed it on the dark granite counter. "Here, buy some real beer. That shit you had tasted like water."

Without so much as a thank you, he walked to the door and left. I couldn't believe that after all this time, he had the nerve to show his face. What baffled me the most was how the hell he managed to find me. After my mom died, I cut all ties with him. She was the only person that meant anything to me. I thought for sure he was never going to show his face again. I couldn't even bring myself to ask him for his consent to let me join the military at seventeen. Forging his signature on the consent form was the best thing I ever did.

CHAPTER THREE

Nikki

When the plane landed at JFK, I wasn't sure what happened to me. My chest got so tight that I couldn't breathe. The only thing I wanted to do was to get off that damn plane. I didn't care that I was being rude by forcing my way to the front of the plane. I was on the verge of hyperventilating, and it was only after I got to the women's bathroom that I realized that I didn't grab my bag from the overhead bin. I knew I couldn't go back on the plane to retrieve it.

Finally able to think straight, I headed out and towards baggage claim. With any luck, my luggage would be waiting for me when I got there. As I was walking in that direction, I kept an eye out for Sly. The last thing I needed was being given the third degree about why I was acting like a psychotic woman.

Reaching the baggage claim area with no sign of Sly, I began looking for my suitcase. It wasn't that hard to find. There weren't too many travelers who had or would even want a pink suitcase. I didn't choose the color because I liked it, I chose it because no one in their right mind would ever purchase a pink luggage set.

After twenty minutes of searching, I came to a couple of conclusions. Either someone stole my suitcase or Sly picked it up and took it with him. Doing the only thing that I could, I reported my luggage as being stolen. Describing the suitcase, TSA finally agreed to look at the camera footage in the baggage claim area. They said I couldn't review the footage with them. Something about privacy and all that, but they did tell me that if someone did pick up my case they would let me know.

Letting them know my flight number and where my luggage was supposed to be, I sat down on one of seats outside the security office. Watching the people walk back and forth in front of me, I sat anxiously waiting for any news on my suitcase. About an hour later, one of the TSA guys called me into the office. He said they might have found who took the pink suitcase and wanted me to verify if I knew the man or not. As soon as I saw Sly on the footage, I took in a breath of relief and let the security officer know that I knew the guy, and it must have been a lack of communication on my part. After thanking them, I hopped into a cab and headed to my apartment.

The TSA officer didn't seem very happy about my admitting I knew Sly. I think he was hoping to see some action or something. As I was riding in the cab, I kept thinking about what Sly must have thought about me and my hysterical behavior. He probably thought that I was a certified nut case the way I flew off the plane. I knew it was only going to be a matter of time before we would be seeing each other again. I needed to come up with some story that he would believe.

I cringed the minute the driver pulled up to my apartment building. Living where I did wasn't the ideal area, but it was the only place I could afford. As I walked up to the building, I noticed some additional artwork on the north wall of the apartment building next to mine. I really needed to find a better place to live. Even with the five locks on my door and the bars on the windows, it still felt like I wasn't safe.

Opening the door to my building, like clockwork the yelling flooded the halls. It was always the same couple. I often wondered why the hell they even stayed together. Unless it was one of those love/ hate relationships.

Trying to tune out the noise, I got to my apartment and began unlocking the door. When I opened the door, there was a card with a logo and writing staring up at me. Bending over, I picked it up from the floor and read that it was from Jagged Edge Security, and Sylvester 'Sly' Capelli was embossed on the front with his contact information. Setting my things down, I pulled my cell from my back pocket and dialed the number on the card.

Not giving him the opportunity to say anything, I asked, straight out, "Where do you live so I can get my suitcase? You had no right to take it."

"What, no 'sorry I left, thanks for getting my suitcase?'" Sly paused, waiting for some kind of reply.

"Don't mess with me, Sly, I am not in the mood. I just spent over an hour at the airport wondering where the hell my suitcase was," I cursed, my patience running thinner by the minute.

"Maybe if you wouldn't have left like a madwoman, I wouldn't have had to take your luggage with me. I didn't know where the hell you went. When you didn't show up, I did the gentlemanly thing and grabbed it for you."

"Well, you shouldn't have. Now, where do you live so I can get it?" I said, even more perturbed.

Finally able to get his address after fifteen minutes of arguing, I called a cab and headed out the door. One thing I knew for sure, Sly would be paying for my cab fare, there and back. After all, it was his fault I had to retrieve it from him. I could have asked him to bring it, but the last thing I needed was for him to begin quizzing me about what happened at the airport. At least by going there, I could get my luggage and leave.

~****~

The minute I got out of the cab and looked up at the glass building, I thought maybe I was at the wrong place. I knew that Jagged Edge Security was the best security company in New York City, but I had no idea that it paid so well. Looking at the address I wrote down, it was definitely the correct address. Paying the driver, I closed the door to the cab and headed inside. As I walked inside, a security guard approached me.

"Can I help you, miss?" he asked with a smile.

"Uh, yeah. I'm here to see Sly Capelli," I answered. I wasn't even sure if the guard knew who I was talking about.

"Yeah, Sly said he was expecting someone, but he didn't say it would be a beautiful woman," the guard answered with a smile. "Go ahead, he is on the twentieth floor, number 2015."

I gave the guard a little smile and walked over to the elevator. As I waited for it to come down, I turned back to the guard to find that he was smiling even bigger with his arms crossed at his chest. Turning my body to face the elevator, so only I could hear, I said, "Pervert." One thing I hated about men twice my age, they always seemed to be hornier than hell.

The elevator skyrocketed upward so fast I didn't even feel it move. Before I knew it, I was on the twentieth floor. Heading in the right direction, I looked at the numbers on the doors until I reached 2015. Knocking lightly, I waited for Sly to answer.

When the door finally opened, I couldn't believe what stood before me. A muscular man, with more muscles than I had ever seen on a man, wearing only a towel around his waist. My month must have dropped a mile. I couldn't get over how absolutely gorgeous he was. All 6'4" of him.

Not knowing what to say, I tried to act unaffected. "Work out much?" I asked as I pushed my way inside the door.

"Come on in," I heard him say sarcastically as I heard him close the door.

"So, I'll just grab my luggage and go," I said sternly.

"Not so fast, darlin'" he began. "Before I give it to you, I think you owe me an explanation."

"I don't owe you anything, Sly. Now if you don't mind, I'd like my suitcase."

His slow movements towards me told me that he wasn't going to give up. He was bound and determined to get the answer he needed. When he got within inches of where I was standing, I lost it completely. The manly scent of musk and something spicy had me wet between my legs. Not only did he look good enough to eat, he also smelled it. All my senses were on arousal overload. It took everything I had not to jump his bones at that very moment.

Trying to back away from him, my efforts were stopped the minute I backed into a wooden support beam. Sly placed his hand against the beam right above my head. Turning my head, I spotted my pink suitcase propped up against the wall with my carry-on bag sitting on top. Given my height, compared to his, it took no effort for me to duck under his arm.

Looking over my shoulder, I ranted behind me, "Catch you later."

The minute I opened the door, I knew there was no way he would be going after me. He should have chosen his attire more wisely. My escape was a lot easier than I thought. I thought for sure he was going to try and charm me with his alpha-male wit. As gorgeous as he was and with how my heart pounded at the sight of him, I knew the best thing for me to do was stay clear of him. I had a funny feeling that if I got any closer to him, it would be really dangerous. Not only because of the things he could do to my deprived body, but also because the truth about myself was not something I wanted to share.

CHAPTER FOUR

Sly

"Damn," I said to myself as I adjusted the towel around my waist that I almost lost completely while trying to go after the biggest pain in my ass. Never had a woman given me the biggest hard-on I've ever had, just by looking at her gorgeous face. Never had a woman been more confusing than Nikki.

I knew it was too late to catch her, but that didn't mean that I couldn't do a little investigation of my own. Walking to my room. I dropped the towel and put on a pair of jeans, commando style, and a dark t-shirt. Grabbing my keys, I headed out to do a little stakeout of my own. Just because she left didn't mean I couldn't watch what she was going to do next.

Putting my Rubicon in reverse, I backed out of my parking spot and headed out of the covered parking garage. Thumping the steering wheel with my thumb to the music playing on the radio, I thought about all the things that didn't make sense with this woman. Even when we were in Kierabali, she didn't act like someone who was nervous about some of the things we asked her to do. It seemed like it was just another ride around the block for her.

Heading into Brooklyn, I took I-278 to Atlantic Avenue, then left on Belmont. I still couldn't understand why anyone would want to live in this area of Brooklyn. Stopping at the end of the block where her apartment building was located, I put my Jeep into park and waited for any movement. Knowing where her apartment was located, I quickly spotted the lights on, along with the bars on her windows that I noticed earlier.

Making myself as comfortable as I could, I sat back and watched. When I was just about ready to give up, I saw someone come out of the building. Even though the person was wearing a hoodie, I could tell that it was

Nikki walking away from the apartment building and heading west. Keeping my distance, I slowly began driving, creeping along, while watching her every move as she continued to walk at a fast pace. I almost thought that she might have made me, but when she went inside an old brick building. I knew I was safe.

Placing the Jeep in park and turning off the engine, I got out and walked across the street to the old building that she entered. I had no idea what this place was, but as soon as I opened the door, it was clear to see that it was some sort of boxing club. The smell of leather and sweat was everywhere. There were also three boxing rings with several punching bags surrounding the perimeter. A couple of guys in the one ring were fighting with no gloves on their hands. The only thing protecting them was the white adhesive tape wrapped around their hands and in between their fingers.

With my eyes peeled, I watched Nikki head to the back of the building, where I assumed the locker rooms were. The majority of the people inside the building were men, so it made me wonder where she would be going.

Keeping a low profile behind a steel beam, I waited for her to appear. Watching the men spar, I realized how good some of them really were. Some of them would make great additions to the security company. Looking around the room, I noticed that there were a few women off in the corner working the speed bags. It was really quite a sight watching them test their quickness.

While I stayed out of sight, Nikki finally entered the large boxing area. She had changed her clothes and was now wearing tight black spandex shorts along with a teal-colored sports bra. This woman was fit. I couldn't keep my eyes off her gorgeous body. Seeing her, it was the first time I had seen so much of her skin. I had a pretty good idea, just by the way she wore her clothing, that she had a gorgeous body under all that material, but this was way beyond that.

Lusting over this woman, I watched her walk over to a black man who was in the far corner of the gym. When she held out her hands, he began wrapping them, first with heavy gauze and then with white adhesive tape.

The way he was wrapping the tape around her hand and in between her fingers, I knew he must have done this a time or two.

Stepping back a couple of paces behind the beam, I couldn't let Nikki see me as she began making her way to the boxing ring closest to where I was standing. As she climbed through the ropes, I watched her make a few air punches to loosen her shoulders. I wasn't sure who she would be fighting, but it had to be one of the girls warming up in the corner of the gym. The only problem with that theory was that they weren't moving. It was only after a man who stood at least six inches taller than her entered the ring that I realized who she was up against. There was no fucking way this guy was going to fight her. I wanted to get her away from him. I knew that given his height and weight, he had a big advantage over her.

With my fist clenched, ready to fight this guy myself, I couldn't believe my eyes. Nikki was actually holding her own. For every punch he threw, she ducked, then gave him a punch of her own. If I hadn't seen it for myself, I would never believe that she would be able to take this guy on. She was so quick on her feet that he didn't know what her next move would be, or if it was going to be her fists making a connection with his body or her foot. It was unreal. I had never seen a woman fight this way before. She was better than most of the guys here.

The more I watched her the more I was amazed by her fighting ability. It made me think that she could probably kick my ass. *"Nah, not quite,"* I thought to myself.

After seeing enough, I headed back to the entrance door and decided it was better to just wait until she finished her workout. As I walked to my car, I kept wondering why a beautiful girl like Nikki would be spending her afternoons in a boxing gym. More than anything, it concerned me how good she was at it. Fighting the way she did wasn't something that she learned overnight. She definitely had been doing this for some time. I needed to find out how long and why.

~****~

I waited half an hour before I decided to enter Nikki's apartment building. I needed to make sure she wouldn't suspect that I had been following her all this time. Giving her plenty of time to get settled, I headed up the three flights of stairs to her apartment. Knocking on her door, I waited for her to answer. I knew that she was inside, but didn't understand what could be taking her so long to open the door.

When she finally came to the door, she had a towel wrapped around her head like some sort of Arabian knight and a very skimpy pajama set on. Unable to stop staring at her, my eyes began scanning her body, starting at the base of those amazing lips all the way down to her perfectly painted toenails.

Clearing her throat to get my attention, she asked, irritated, "Are you going to stand there and gawk all day or are you coming in?"

Knowing an invitation when I heard one, I

stepped past her into her small, but very clean apartment. Taking in the surroundings, there was something that just didn't seem right about her place. For one thing, there was hardly any furniture, and for another, there weren't any pictures on the walls. They were as bare as a padded cell. There was no evidence of who she was and what she liked. It looked more like a place to sleep and nothing more.

Taking a seat on the couch, I watched her approach me and take a seat on the floor in front of me. It was kind of silly, really, knowing that there was plenty of room beside me for her to sit.

Crossing her legs, Indian style, she asked, "So what are you doing here, Sly?"

Taking in a breath, I replied, "What is going on with you, Nikki? Even though we haven't known each other very long, I can guarantee that something is up with you."

"I don't know what you're talking about, Sly.

What's it to you anyway?" she countered.

"I think you know exactly what I am talking about, and it is everything to me," I retorted.

"Well, you don't need to worry about me, I can take care of myself. Always have."

"I don't doubt that," I began, sliding down the couch so that I was on the floor sitting next to her. "Something is going on with you and I think you may need some help."

The minute she looked up at me, I knew it was a cry for help. Those beautiful brown eyes took me inside to witness the pain she was holding back. Unable to resist them any longer, I dipped my head lower, until our lips met. Even though there was a hint of salt on them, they were the softest lips I had ever set my mouth on.

When she didn't resist, I pushed my tongue between her parted lips, allowing me to feel the warmth inside. As our tongues mingled together, soft moans of pleasure vibrated between them. Deepening the kiss, I pulled her closer and lifted her small frame off the floor and onto my lap. Nikki's hands wrapped around my shoulders, pulling me even further inside the sweet depths of her warmth.

Her hands began snaking through my hair, making me want to take her right there. Placing my hand along her back, I slowly guided her backwards until her back rested on the floor. Towering over her with her legs wrapped around me, I lowered myself to her and kissed her gently on her neck, breathing in her scent at the same time. I needed to have more of her.

Tugging the bottom of her pajama top, I lifted it up over her head, exposing her very feminine lacy bra. Watching her breathing getting heavier, I placed my mouth at the top of her chest where I knew her rapid heartbeat could be felt and gently worked my way down her body, leaving soft petal-like kisses one after the other. Reaching between her ample breasts, finding the clasp of her bra, I unhooked it, revealing the smooth, silky mounds of her soft flesh. Placing one hand over her breast, I began caressing the soft skin while continuing my way down her body. Her skin was so silky soft, I couldn't get enough of the feel as my mouth absorbed every inch of her.

When her back began to arch, I knew that she was reeling in the pleasure I was giving her. Kissing and sucking her glorious skin was all I wanted to do. When I got to her tight stomach I dipped my tongue inside her cute belly button, driving her even closer to the point of pure ecstasy. With my free hand, I lowered her bottoms. With no effort, her bottoms were off and the only item of clothing remaining on her gorgeous body were her tiny lacy underwear, which should have been called 'barely there to drive a man crazy' panties.

Nikki's moans continued to echo in the small apartment, sending a surge of fire to my already hard dick. I wasn't sure how much longer I could hold off. I only knew that I needed to be inside this woman. Trying to remove my own jeans, I heard her small, soft voice say, "Do you have a Johnny?"

I had never heard a condom called that before, but I knew exactly what she was asking of me. "Yeah, baby, I got you covered," I replied, pulling my wallet out from my back pocket.

With my cock sheathed, I was more than ready to consume her. Positioning my cock at her entrance, I slowly began moving inside her. As her warmth coated me, I could feel my cock pulsating within her tight walls, causing it to get harder and harder. The way she felt was like bathing on a sunny day and getting an ice cream sundae all at once. The more I pushed, the tighter she gripped me. Her entrance was so tight, I was certain I was hurting her. It was almost like fucking a virgin. Raising my head, I looked into her hooded eyes. "Are you okay, baby?"

"Yeah, keep going, I want to feel more of you," she muttered.

Her arms wrapped around my shoulders and I could feel the grip of her hands on my skin. As her hips rose upward, I knew that she was close. Lowering to my elbows, I kissed her gently on the lips, feeling her moans of pleasure vibrating between us. Her grip tightened as I pushed even further inside. The heavens above must have heard her scream of ecstasy because a clap of thunder echoed in the darkness as her body let go with such force that my own release consumed me. Our bodies melted together as one as I took her once again, leaving her body and mind fully satisfied.

CHAPTER FIVE

Nikki

I had no idea what happened last night. All I knew was that I couldn't let it happen again. As good as it felt, I couldn't let this man get close to me. Not now, not while my life was in someone else's control. The best thing I could do was to chalk this off as a one-night stand and move on.

Looking over my shoulder at Sly lying there in all his perfect gorgeousness, I pushed from the bed to take a much-needed shower. As I lifted off the bed, I felt a soft grip on my hand. As I took in his magnificent body, he asked, with a gruff tone, "Where are you going, beautiful?"

"I need to shower," I replied.

"What time is it, anyway?" he asked.

"It's almost six. I have things I need to do today."

"You go take your shower and I'll get us some breakfast," he yawned, throwing the covers from his body, exposing the hard lines of his muscles.

"I usually don't eat breakfast, but coffee would be nice."

"Then coffee it is."

I could have stood there all day watching him, but I knew what we had and it had to end. Walking to the door, I took one last look at him before I headed to the bathroom. I knew I didn't have much time before he would be back. I needed to shower fast and make sure I wasn't here when he got back.

~****~

After taking the quickest ten-minute shower I had

ever taken, I hurried and got dressed. Twenty minutes later I was dressed and on my way out the door before Sly got back. Grabbing my cell, I stuffed it in my pocket along with some cash, and I locked my door and headed out.

As I exited the building there was one thing I knew I needed to take care of, and that was to find out if I still had a job. It had been three weeks since I had contacted the Happy Cow. For all I knew, my job would be gone and some other bimbo with big boobs would be the new barista.

Hailing a cab, which I really couldn't afford, I headed to Midtown. Twenty bucks later, I was dropped off in front of the small coffee shop. Nothing had changed since I left, except maybe the new special for the day, '*Tall latte with your choice of a Blueberry Scone or a Blueberry Muffin for $7.99,*' which Erin had written in neon colors so it could be seen blocks away. She was always doing stuff like that to attract customers.

It was still early enough, just after seven, and the

Happy Cow hadn't opened yet for its rush of coffee drinkers. It was the perfect time to find out what my fate would be. Unlocking the door with the key, I entered the shop, re-locking the door before I headed to the back of the shop. I spotted Erin sitting at her desk going through the sales receipts that I assumed were from the day before. I remember when I first got hired, she told me that coffee was her life; growing up in Brazil, her family owned a coffee plantation. Even though she was pretty young when they sold their home and moved to the States, she would never forget her countless days she spent working the plantation and preparing the beans for processing.

Knocking on the door, I waited for her to see me. "Entrar," she said, without so much as a gaze my way.

Opening the door, I knew the minute she looked up that she was surprised to see me. Sitting in the chair next to her cluttered desk, I said in a timid voice, "Hey."

"We've missed you," Erin said with a smile.

"I know, it's been super crazy the past few weeks," I replied

"Well, you're back now, hopefully to stay for a while. I kept your position open. Had you come a week later it would have been filled," she stated.

"So I still have my job?" I asked in disbelief.

"Barely."

"Thanks, Erin. I'll get my apron and get to work."

This couldn't have been a better day for me. I still had my job and Erin wasn't angry that I didn't contact her all those weeks I was gone. Grabbing an apron from the hook where all of the newly laundered aprons hung, I placed the strap over my head and cinched the tie around my waist. It was getting close to opening time and it looked like everything was already in place for the day.

Taking the keys from my pocket, I walked over to the door and unlocked it. It didn't surprise me to find that

Sly was waiting to enter on the other side. My perfect day just turned into a shit day by the way he was glaring at me through the glass. I could have kept the door locked and walked away, but I knew there was no time like the present to face what I knew was going to be an ass chewing.

Pulling the door open, I turned and walked back to the counter, but not before addressing his presence. "How did you find me, Sly?"

Without so much as *"Hey, how are you. Where the fuck did you go?"* he glared back at me before settling his hands on the small checkout counter. Turning his body, there was that glare again, only this time it was followed by his anger. "What the fuck, Nikki? You knew I was going to be right back. Why would you leave like that?"

"Yeah, well… you took too long and I needed to be here," I mumbled. "You still haven't answered me."

"And… you couldn't have picked up your phone

and let me know you needed to take off."

"I was in a hurry and didn't have time." My explanation was beginning to go from bad to worse.

"Not believing it, Nikki," he confessed.

Rolling my eyes at him, I pushed past him to take my place behind the coffee bar. Busying myself with preparing the espresso machine, I heard a big sigh from Sly. I knew he was getting frustrated as hell, but I couldn't let him know the real reason for not being at my apartment when he returned. As much as I knew that I wasn't any good for him, it didn't mean that I didn't want him.

Throwing his hands up in the air, I watched as he headed to the entrance of the coffee shop. I couldn't let him leave this way. "Sly," I called out waiting for him to turn. "I'm sorry. Things are just really complicated in my life right now."

"I get it, Nikki. I know when I am being blown

off," he admitted.

"It's not like that," I corrected.

"It seems pretty clear to me," he paused, shaking his head. "Catch you on the flip side."

The small bell rang as he opened the door. Just like that, he was gone. I couldn't let him just leave like that without a better explanation. Rounding the counter, I jogged to the door and opened it. He must have heard that damn bell, because he stopped in his tracks and turned to face me.

Lowering my head, I walked up to him and said softly, "Can you please not be this way? Everything is just so... so messed up right now. I like being with you. I just need to work some stuff out."

"What's going on with you, Nikki? What's going on in that pretty little head of yours that you can't tell me?" Sly questioned softly, placing his hand on my cheek.

As I looked up at him, I knew he was concerned for me. When his head lowered, I wanted to back away from him, but my heart took over and I allowed him to place a tender kiss on my wanting lips. It didn't matter that we were kissing in the middle of the sidewalk and being stared at by the people passing by, some of which were whistling as they walked past us.

When our kiss broke, my body was on fire. The way Sly kissed me left me wanting even more, but PDA in the middle of the sidewalk wasn't the place to get my fill of this gorgeous guy. Lifting my chin, I looked up at him with lustful eyes. Sly leaned over and gently kissed my forehead before saying, "We'll talk when you get off."

Nodding my head, I turned back to the shop, controlling my need to look back and watch him get into his Jeep. No sooner than I got behind the counter, the coffee shop began filling with patrons wanting their morning fix. There was one thing good about being busy, at least I wouldn't be thinking about Sly.

~****~

Once again, I was ducking out before Sly had the chance to quiz me about what was going on. I knew he would be back, but I didn't want to wait for him to show up.

My body was sore and achy from my workout yesterday and my first day back to work. I knew I needed a lot more training, but the way I felt, I nixed the workout and decided to go home and relax; after all, tomorrow was another day. I wasn't sure what was going to happen in the next couple of days, but I suspected that soon one of Carlos Giordano's men would be paying me a visit. Carlos wasn't a very nice man. Ever since I was thirteen, he made sure that his investment was working hard making every cent he could. That investment was me. All 50k's of it.

Day after day, I worked my ass off so I could get out from under this evil man. I could have told Carlos to go fuck himself, but there was one thing he knew that no one else did, and that one thing gave him the control he needed to keep me making his dirty money for him. I had paid that man three times over, but that didn't matter. As long as I was still alive and able to fight, he was going to claim every dime he could from me.

Locking the door, I walked the few blocks to the subway. My tips for the day pretty much sucked. It didn't help that I was crabby all day after my run-in with Sly. And now I was ditching him again to avoid being interrogated.

Reaching the turnstile, I quickly swiped my Metrocard and headed to the train platform. It didn't take long before the train pulled up and the doors opened. Even though I didn't care for taking the subway, it was still the least expensive way to travel. A taxi would have been much better. At least I would have been home sooner and wouldn't have had to deal with all the strange people that ride the subway. I think that every year it was getting worse and worse. I have a sneaky suspicion that soon there will be a subway patrol assigned to make sure the people riding them are kept safe.

Reaching the end of the line, I walked the few blocks to my home. This was another thing that I hated. By the time I got off work at night, it was dark, and walking the few blocks to my apartment building in the neighborhood that I lived in wasn't exactly the best scenario. Even though I had never been attacked by anyone, there was definitely that risk.

Reaching my building, I recognized the red Rubicon parked out in front. Stopping beside it, I took a quick look inside to see that Sly wasn't sitting behind the driver's seat. That could only mean one thing, he had to be waiting for me inside. Bowing my head in defeat, I knew I couldn't stay out in the dark and wait until he left. It was time that I manned up to face the music.

It looked liked the elevator had finally been fixed, but I chose instead to walk up the three flights of stairs to my apartment. It would give me some time to think about what kind of story I was going to tell Sly during our talk. Climbing the last step, I looked down the hall to see that Sly was standing with his body leaning against the wall.

His attention was on his cell phone, so he hadn't seen me yet. I could have just sat on the stairs and waited for him to leave, but eventually he would be coming my way, and I would be caught and would have to come up with another explanation as to why I was sitting in the stairwell. Taking in a much-needed breath, I held my head high and walked toward him.

His focus turned from his phone to me in an instant. Before he could give me the riot act, I jumped in first. "I can explain."

"And you will. All of it, Nikki," he said sternly, like I was a teenager who had just been caught staying out too late.

"What is it to you anyway, Sly? It's not like we are committed to each other?" I argued.

"Are you kidding me, Nikki? We just fucked each other less than twenty-four hours ago and that is all you can say?" he remarked.

"Yeah, well, aren't you guys accustomed to one-night stands?" I questioned.

"Is that what you think that was? A one-night stand."

I could feel the anger in his tone as he began pacing the hall, running his hands through his hair like it was the worst thing I could have said to him. I had never seen a man react the way he did. Normally it was the other way around. *Who would have thought that Sly, of all people, took our little roll in the hay as something more?*

As he paced further from the door, I knew I wouldn't be able to get inside before he made it back. One thing I didn't count on was him reaching out and grabbing my arm. The pull caused my body to crash into his. His hands trailed down my back before they settled on the globes of my ass. Just as quickly as he had my body pressed against his, he had me off the floor and up against the wall next to my apartment door. Before I could say anything, he demanded, "Keys."

Holding out the hand that was grasping the keys, he took them from me and expertly located the right key and placed it inside the lock. With my body still pressed tightly between him and the wall, he opened the door and pushed it open. Maneuvering us through the door, he bumped it closed with his back and then turned our bodies, pressing mine up against the door. There was a tingle in the pit of my stomach. The way he was able to do the things he did, without the slightest break in our connection, was sexy as hell. He was not only in charge of the situation, he also became in charge of what my body was doing every minute he held me close to him.

Lifting my chin, he looked at me in such a way, he was telling me that he was in control and there was nothing I could do to stop it. When his mouth fell upon mine, at that moment, I couldn't, nor did I want him to stop. The sweet taste of mint on his tongue filled my mouth as we mingled together. I could feel every nerve in my body begin to come alive as the heat between us began to ignite.

Needing more of him, I slipped my hand between

our bodies and placed my hand over the hard pulsating of his masculinity. He was like a rocket, ready to blast off, and I was his launching pad. It was very clear how much we craved each other. Changing the position of our bodies once again, Sly adjusted his hold on me and began heading to my bedroom. Gently lowering me on the bed, he broke free from our embrace long enough to pull off my black leggings and lacy pink thong underwear. Removing his own pants, he took out his wallet and pulled out a condom. Ripping the package with his teeth, I watched him expertly roll it onto his cock with one hand. It was the sexiest thing I had ever seen.

With his body hovering over mine, he licked his middle finger and placed it between my slick folds. When his finger entered, my body jolted from the sensation of his finger inside me as well as from the movement he was delivering to my sweet spot. Just when I was at the point of letting go, he pulled from me. Taking hold of my ankles, he held them gently and kissed the inside of each one before flipping me onto my stomach. Reaching underneath my stomach, he guided my hips upward, causing my butt to lift higher. With a gentle thrust, his shaft entered me, sending my body soaring with so much pleasure that I screamed his name over and over until my voice was lost and I could no longer make a sound.

Filling me completely, it only took a few more thrusts before Sly was met with his release. Deep penetrating moans of satisfaction echoed inside the small room before his body fell upon me. Kissing me lightly on the forehead, he pushed off and headed to the bathroom.

When Sly returned from the bathroom, he pulled my body close to his. I was beginning to have feelings for him that I couldn't just push away. All I could think about was how much trouble I could cause him if he knew the truth about who I really was. With my mind totally spent fighting the "what if's," I finally gave in to my exhaustion, and closed my eyes.

CHAPTER SIX
Sly

While I laid in bed thinking of nothing else but the best sex ever, my mind was distracted by the soft sound of Nikki snoring beside me. It wasn't really that loud, but had me thinking about what little I really knew about the woman beside me. I not only had one mind-blowing orgasm with her, but two. Starting tomorrow, I was going to make it my priority to find out who she really was, and why she was spending most of her evenings at the run-down boxing gym located in a not-so-great neighborhood. But mostly, I was going to find out if she would agree to let me find her a better place to live, away from her current residence and the risk of being mugged, or worse, killed.

Morning was fast approaching and I had yet to

sleep a wink. Too many things were running through my mind. Rolling over onto my side, I propped my head on my hand and watched as Nikki laid still beside me. The only movement was the rise and fall of her chest as she inhaled and exhaled each breath. Her soft snoring seized about an hour ago and was exchanged for what I assumed was a bad dream of some sort. I almost felt the need to wake her, but I held back while I watched her work through it. The way she was moving around on the bed, I could tell that she was dreaming about being held or possibly attacked. The only name that escaped her mouth was 'Mom.' It made me wonder what could have happened to her that she would be calling out to her mom.

The light of morning was finally coming through the window, leaving a shadow of the bars on the wall. It made no sense why Nikki would feel the need to have them, especially since there was no way inside the window from the outside. I could understand trying to be safe from the trouble outside, especially in this neighborhood, but she definitely went overboard with the bars across the windows.

Even though it was still early, I found it hard to
get any sleep. Pushing from the bed, I decided to search
out some coffee. Pulling on my jeans, I grabbed my cell
from her tiny nightstand and headed to the kitchen to see
what I could find. As I searched through her cupboards, I
wasn't able to find anything resembling a coffee maker,
coffee, or even coffee cups. To be perfectly honest, I
found it rather odd that her cupboards were quite bare.
The only thing I was able to find was one set of
tableware, which pretty much consisted of a plate, bowl,
and small plate. There weren't even any pots or pans used
for cooking. Everyone had at least a pot and a frying pan,
but Nikki had nothing.

Determined to satisfy my coffee fix, I removed
the keys from my pocket and got the things I needed. Just
as I got to the door, I remembered the last time I left
Nikki's apartment. There was no way I was going to
come back to an empty apartment. Searching around the
room, I spotted the keys to her apartment on the small
table in front of the couch. Picking them up, I once again
walked to the front door.

It was no surprise to find that the same voices were yelling at each other again. I wondered if the other residents of the building were as tired of it as I was. I should have intervened, but I was currently on a mission to get my coffee and get back. Blocking out the noise, I headed down the remaining two flights of stairs to my Jeep, which was parked across the street. Given the neighborhood Nikki lived in, I prayed that my Jeep was still in one piece.

My Jeep was good, but this was the last time I would be parking it in this area. It was time Nikki had a change of residence. Pulling my phone from my pocket, I found Lou's contact number and punched send. Lou was one of the guys from Jagged Edge Security that I worked with. Over the years we had gotten quite close. His childhood was much like mine, with only one difference: both his parents were caught in the crossfire of a deal gone bad. His dad was part of the Mob as well, only his dad got out before he was born. Lou was young when his parents died, but he was pretty sure it was related to his dad's early dealings with the Mafia. He, of course, could never prove it.

"Hey, Lou. Any news on that apartment you cousin has available?" I asked.

"Yeah, I was just about ready to call you. Your friend can have it by the end of the week. He just needs some time to give it a fresh coat of paint and get the carpets cleaned. Does your friend prefer any specific color other than white?" Lou asked.

"Don't know, but I wouldn't go with white. Maybe something a little darker."

~****~

By the time I returned to Nikki's apartment, I had a shiny new coffee maker, a large container of coffee, filters, and two coffee mugs that displayed 'His' and 'Hers' in black letters. I hadn't noticed it until I got to Nikki's door, but there wasn't any yelling coming from the second floor. Either they got tired of yelling at each other or someone finally said something. No matter, it was nice to have the peace and quiet. Pulling Nikki's apartment key from my pocket, I unlocked the door.

I decided to check on Nikki before I made us each a cup of coffee. When I got to her room, she was no longer in bed. Turning to the bathroom, the door was open, which told me she wasn't there either. "Shit," I cursed out loud, knowing she once again left me alone. As I was heading back to the kitchen, I heard the front door open, and Nikki was on the other side. She was wearing a pair of pajama shorts and a t-shirt which left nothing to the imagination, the way her nipples were pressed against the thin fabric.

Walking toward her, I could see that something was off. Lifting her chin, she had a little swelling under her eye and her lip had a tiny cut on it. Taking another look at her body, trying not to focus on her beautiful tits, her knuckles were red and swollen as well.

"What the hell happened to you, Nikki?" I asked, confused.

"Just something that I should have done a long time ago," she admitted.

"I would say by looking at you, it was more than just something. You mind telling me where you went?" I asked, lifting her hands and examining the damage.

"I put an end to the yelling and screaming once and for all. Surly you noticed it when you came back. Where did you go?" she asked.

"Did you know you don't have anything in this apartment? It's like your only purpose here is to sleep."

"I'm not like you, Sly. There are some luxuries that I can't afford, so I make the best I can with what I have," she replied defensively.

I knew it was more than that as I directed her to the kitchen to show her what she no longer had to go without.

"You shouldn't have done that," she said, looking

at the coffee maker and coffee supplies.

"Yeah, I should. If I'm going to be spending any time with you, I need to have coffee in the morning."

Rolling her eyes, she said, "Well, then I guess you won't be spending any time with me, because I can't accept it."

Before she could leave the room, I took her by the arm and leaned over. Whispering softly, I said, "You sure about that?" before I placed my lips on hers, taming her sarcastic attitude.

Her mouth soon parted and my tongue went inside her inner warmth. I tried to be careful with her, but my need to take her overtook any gentleness I intended to give her. Grasping her tight ass, I lifted her up on the small counter. Her moans of surprise vibrated between us. Taking the hem of her t-shirt, I lifted it up over her head, exposing her firm breasts. Breaking our kiss, I lowered my head to her nipple, sucking and licking until it came to a hard peak. Moving to the other side, I gave her other nipple the same attention. I knew my playful indulgence was only the beginning of what I was going to give her.

As I teased and sucked her taut nipple, I could feel her body beginning to give in to my touch. Lowering my hands down her silky body, I lifted her slightly off the counter, just high enough to remove her bottoms. I needed to feel the warmth of her wrapped around my throbbing cock. Reaching behind me, I pulled out my wallet, only to find I didn't have what I was looking for. I could have kicked myself in the ass for not coming prepared. In a hushed whisper, I said, "No condom, babe."

I thought Nikki pushed off the counter to get away from me, but instead she lowered to her knees and began working the buckle of my belt and then the zipper of my jeans. Tugging them down my legs, she began massaging the base of my cock with one hand while she milked the length with the other. Whatever she was doing made me want more. When she lowered her mouth and took me between her velvety lips, I just about exploded then. Even though she hadn't taken the full length of my cock inside her mouth, what she was doing with her tongue had me reeling with pleasure. There was nothing I wanted more than to be deep inside her.

Pressing her tongue against the base of my cock, it took everything I had not to buckle. The way she was working me, it was almost as good as being lodged deep inside her. Almost ready to explode, Nikki pulled her mouth from my rock-hard cock and stood. I wasn't sure what happened, but her lips fell to mine and a soft whisper left her lips. "Take me, Sly, I need you inside me."

"I don't have a condom, baby," I whispered with regret.

"It's okay, trust me," she vowed.

Trusting her completely, I turned her body so that her upper body was leaning over the counter. It was the sexiest thing I had ever seen. The way her ass looked, I could have fucked that little pucker in a second. *Maybe another day.* Positioning my cock to her entrance, I slowly began working it inside her tight pussy. Inch by inch, I eased my way in, deeper and deeper. The strength of her walls bored down on my shaft, causing an unbelievable feeling that was beyond words to describe. Never had a woman's pussy felt so good. "God, baby, you feel so good," I grunted as I moved further inside her tight channel. Never had I fucked a woman without protection, but there was something about Nikki that made it worth the risk.

Placing my hands on her hips, I felt her body push against mine as I pushed deeper inside her. I loved seeing the contour of her back as I fucked her from behind. Moving my hands from her hips, I slid them up to the indentation of her waist and then to the soft, firm mounds of her breasts. Taking one in each hand, I began caressing and gently squeezing them while taking her hard buds between my fingers. I could feel the moisture building between her legs the more I tightened my grip on her nipples. Removing my hand, I snaked my fingers through her long hair and pulled gently on her head. Leaning closer over her body, I whispered, "Come for me, baby."

I knew the minute my demand left my lips, her sweet honey would be coating my cock. Before my last thrust landed, my own pleasure erupted as my seed spilled from my naked cock into her tight channel.

CHAPTER SEVEN

Nikki

When I couldn't find the keys to my apartment, I knew that Sly had taken them. It only made sense that he would, considering I had left him with no explanation two times before. I had to do something about the yelling that was going on below me. Enough was enough. I had put up with it since the day I moved into this dump, four months ago, to be exact. Day in and day out, I listened to them fight over things that really didn't make much sense. *Who fights over leaving the lid off of the toothpaste, anyway?*

Grabbing the first thing I could, I slipped on my pajama bottoms and a t-shirt. Closing the door behind me, I headed down the flight of stairs to apartment 206 to finally put an end to the fighting. When I got to the door,

I took a deep breath before knocking on the door. When the door opened and a scrawny form of a man answered, I knew this was going to be a cinch. What I didn't expect was a woman who looked like she was healing from a previous beating coming up behind him.

Pulling my shoulders back, I told them both how it was. "You guys have been at each other for four months now, maybe even longer. There are other people that live in this dump that would like a little peace and quiet. Could you please, and I'm saying this in a nice way, shut the fuck up and stop the fucking yelling."

It must not have been what he wanted to hear, because the scrawny little turd's fist came across my face before I had a chance to move out of the way. Looking up at him as I wiped the drop of blood coming from my lip, I gave him a one-two and watched as he nearly fell on his woman, who was struggling to keep him upright.

Pulling him towards me by the collar of his shirt, I looked him straight in the eye and said in an even tone, "The yelling stops now, and if that pretty face of your woman has any more bruising, my fists hitting your face is going to be the least of your worries."

Pretending to come at him again, I cocked my fist back only to leave him with a small pat against his cheek. By the way he jerked back, I was pretty sure he got the message. Turning away from the door, I waited until I heard it close before I looked to the sky and said "Allelujah," in a soft whisper. I wasn't sure what got into me. All I knew was that I saw something in that man that I had seen before. It was the devil and he needed to be stopped.

I didn't think I was gone that long, but unfortunately for me, Sly had come back to the apartment before I could clean myself up. The look on his face when I opened the door was one I had also seen before. It was the same look my mom gave me before I collapsed in her arms when I was fourteen. Only this time I knew how to survive. I wasn't that innocent girl who took everything that came at her without so much as a fight.

~****~

Trying to wrap my head around what just happened, I poured a small portion of shampoo in my hand. The way Sly and I just went at it in the kitchen was like a couple of teenagers with raging hormones going wild. I wasn't even thinking when I told Sly to trust me. I was pretty sure he was clean, but that was still no excuse to have sex unprotected. My chances of getting pregnant were next to impossible, but there was still that small chance that it could happen.

Everything about this man clouded my judgement. I couldn't think straight. The minute he placed his lips on mine, my inner self was held hostage to his touch. I knew I couldn't have a long-term relationship with Sly. It was like giving him over to Carlos myself. The minute Carlos found out about Sly, he would use it against me to get what he needed.

Rinsing the shampoo from my hair, I decided then that no matter how much I wanted this man, I needed to end this thing with him. Speaking of the sexy man himself, there he was, standing in all of his naked gorgeousness. My thoughts of letting this man go just flew out the window as he stepped inside the small shower, pressing his hard body next to mine. Grabbing the bath sponge from its cradle, he took my vanilla-scented body wash and squeezed a small amount onto the sponge. Gently massaging it between his fingers until enough lather was built up, he softly began rubbing the sponge across my body, beginning at my shoulder and down my arm. Reaching the valley between my breasts, he lingered there while caressing each breast with tender loving care. The touch he had on my body only brought more wetness between my legs.

Dipping his head, he placed light kisses on my shoulder and continued to the base of my neck, sending my body even further into the land of complete bliss. Everything he was doing I knew I needed to stop, but I could only stand there under his power and let him have his way with me. My body was his. No more could I fight the pleasure my body hungered for. No more did I have the will to say 'stop.'

Turning my body towards him, I pressed my taut nipples to his firm chest. I needed to feel him as much as he wanted to feel me. Taking the sponge from his hand, I placed one hand on his broad shoulder while gliding the soapy sponge down his chest. Before the soap could cover too much of him, I lowered my mouth to his erect nipple and began kissing and sucking, feeling the beating of his heart beneath my hand as it rested on his chest. Just the feel of his flexing muscles under my hand had me going crazy with need for him.

Lifting my body closer to him, our lips joined as one before I could finish my exploration of his perfect body. Not even the fact that the shower was only meant for one person stopped him from taking what he needed. As he slowly entered me, I couldn't help but want more of him. His strokes were so smooth and gentle that every time he moved deeper inside me, I wanted him that much more. Reaching the ultimate freedom, my body shook, delivering the most euphoric release I had ever shed. Just as my body began to relax, Sly was met with his own release, muttering softly, "Fucking amazing."

~****~

My body was totally drained from the two bouts of the most incredible sex I ever had. I had no idea that it could be so wonderful. Coming back to reality, I needed to get my mind around what was happening. I was really beginning to have feelings for this Sly, which I knew I absolutely couldn't afford to have.

Quickly drying off my body and getting dressed, I headed to the kitchen where Sly was pouring us a cup of coffee, Grabbing the mug with 'Hers' written on the side, I said in a serious voice. "I don't mean to kick you out, but I have a lot of things I need to do today."

With one of his 'what the fuck' looks, he replied, "Just like that. After the mind-blowing sex we just had, you're pushing me away."

"Look, Sly, here's the deal. I have a lot going on right now, and having a clingy guy with insecurities is not my thing. Yeah, the sex was great, but that's all it was," I lied.

"I'm out of here. And just for the record, I have

never been clingy or insecure," he pointed out.

Gathering his things, he opened the door and left before I could take back what I said. Taking a moment to decide whether or not to go after him, I rose from my seat, opened the door, and jogged down the stairs, hoping to catch him before he was gone. Pushing the door to the building with full force, I watched Sly's Jeep pull away from the curb. It was too late, he drove off, and I didn't have time to apologize for what I said. I didn't even have my phone with me to call him.

Feeling totally defeated, I turned to head back to my apartment. Walking along the sidewalk, I noticed a black Escalade pull up to the curb. I couldn't see who was inside because of the dark windows. When the window lowered and a hand slowly gestured for me to come closer, I knew it could only be one person calling me over: Carlos Giordano. The one man who brought nothing but bad news my way.

Stepping up to the window, I saw the disgusting man sitting inside like this was no more than a friendly visit. "Nikki, how is my little Firefly?"

"What do you want, Carlos?" I asked with a seething breath.

"Just checking in on my investment, and to make sure you're keeping up with your training. I've been a little concerned with your actions lately. Taking off with no word was not a wise move. I hope you haven't forgotten your obligations," he advised.

"Don't worry, you'll get what's owed to you. Soon you'll be fully paid and out of my life for good."

"Now, Nikki, no need to be so ugly. I kind of like our little connection. I would hate to lose that."

"Yeah, well the feeling is definitely not mutual," I hissed before turning away from him and back to my safe haven.

Grabbing my arm before I could make my escape, he ordered, "I suggest you watch your tone with me. I might find it necessary to add an additional incentive to make up for your rude behavior."

Watching the Escalade drive off, I flipped him the bird. I thought for sure I was in for it when the brake lights came on, but instead the SUV continued down the street. *God, how I hated that man.*

CHAPTER EIGHT

Sly

I wasn't sure what had got into my little spitfire, but I knew there was no way Nikki meant what she said. The heat that was exchanged between us was not that of someone who wasn't looking for anything. I wasn't going to let this thing we had between us go. It felt too good. Too right. There was no way I could let a feeling like that go.

As I pulled around the corner, I knew something bad was going down between whoever was in the black SUV and Nikki. Even though the conversation lasted a few minutes between them, I knew the second the hand reached out and grabbed her arm that the guy doing the grabbing was not willing to let Nikki go. I only wished I had parked on the other side of the street so I could get a clear view of the plate. I guess getting the first three digits was better than not having anything at all.

Pulling out my cell, I decided to give Peter a call to see if he could find out anything on the partial plate I got. Certainly there weren't too many black Escalades with the first four digits 'FCA-5' on them.

When I was finished giving Peter the information to check out, I sat back and waited for something to happen, namely Nikki leaving her apartment building. I was getting restless, but she finally appeared after I waited for about an hour. Watching her head down the sidewalk, I waited until she was far enough away until I could stay a safe distance behind her so she wouldn't suspect that I was following her. Based on the direction she was walking, I had a pretty good idea where she was going.

Parking across the street, I watched as she entered the gym. Trying to be patient, I sat in the Jeep for about fifteen minutes before I decided it was long enough. When I opened the door to the gym, Nikki was already in the boxing ring, sparring with another female about the same height and build as her. Leaning against a cement post, I stayed hidden as I watched them go back and forth popping blow after blow at each other. Nikki was landing most of her blows while the other girl missed most of hers. It didn't surprise me, the way Nikki moved around, taking full control of the area. She was quick on her feet, ducking and swaying with full concentration, anticipating when and where the other girl's punches and kicks would happen.

Watching Nikki was like nothing I had ever seen before. It was ten times better than watching an MMA fight on television. Fully engrossed in the two of them fighting, I didn't notice the muscular black man step behind me.

"Enjoying the view?" he asked, crossing his arms across his thick chest.

"Yeah. Who's the girl fighting Nikki?" I replied.

"That would be Carly Burns. She's one of the best

MMA fighters here, aside from Nikki. You interested in a little action?" he asked.

"Action?" I questioned.

"Yeah. There's a fight coming up next Saturday. Supposed to be the fight of the season. Nikki is favored to win 15 to 1. She's fighting an undefeated fighter from Chicago by the name of Black Jewel."

"Wait, are you saying Nikki is fighting this woman?" I clarified, not believing what he just said.

"You got it. It's taking place at the old refinery. So do you want in on the action or not?"

A hundred bucks later, I was in and out of money. I still couldn't believe that Nikki would be involved in illegal underground fighting. This was something that was normally seen among men, but to have two women going at it was unheard of. After I paid the guy, I remained behind the concrete pillar, watching Nikki take this girl out. With my attention on Nikki doing her footwork on the other side of the ring, I didn't see two men approach the ring until they climbed over the ropes to assist Carly, who was out cold. For this being a practice fight, Nikki was definitely letting off some steam.

When Nikki was satisfied that Carly was okay, she ducked under the top rope and headed to the locker room. The minute she was out of view, I knew it was my chance to leave before Nikki saw me.

Driving to my place, I still couldn't get a handle on why Nikki would feel the need to fight. I totally got that given where she was currently living, she needed some sort of protection against the hoodlums living there. Taking my cell, I needed to find out if there was any information on the partial plate I gave to Peter. I knew it had only been an hour since I spoke to him, but this information couldn't wait.

"Hey Peter, any word on that partial plate?" I asked impatiently.

"Not yet, bro. It's going to take some time to match what you gave us to the SUV," Peter replied.

"I know, I was hoping you would have something," I paused. "Hey, Peter, do you know anything about underground fighting?"

"Not much. Only that it's illegal as hell. I do know one thing, most of those fights are run by Mafia-related entities. Why you ask?"

"No particular reason. Just wondering. Let me know as soon as you get anything on that plate." I said, ending the call.

I knew I probably should have let Peter in on what I found out about Nikki, but I needed more facts before I said anything. Mostly, the reason behind Nikki fighting in the first place.

~****~

So the best way to get to a woman was to woo her

with all the things women liked: chocolate, flowers, dinner, and a night out on the town. The only problem was, I wasn't sure if Nikki was the kind of woman who would be interested in any of those things. I decided my best bet would be to introduce them one at a time. I just didn't know which one would work the best. Maybe I was thinking along the wrong lines. Maybe a Yankees game would be more suitable for her.

Slipping on my jacket, I headed out to check out the new place Lou's cousin had available. I had already put down the deposit of six hundred dollars just to hold it until I could check it out myself. Lou was already waiting outside the apartment building when I pulled up. Even though the building had its own parking garage, I thought it best to just park along the street.

Shaking his hand in a brotherly way, I gave him a half hug and said, "Thanks for talking to your cousin, bro. I really appreciate it."

"I think it will work out for your girlfriend. What's the deal with you two anyway?" Lou inquired.

"Long story, bro," I confessed.

"Well, she must be pretty special for you to fork over the dough to secure this place."

"Yeah, I guess you could say that." I didn't want to elaborate any more on what Lou said. All I knew was she was worth helping. Maybe getting her this apartment would be the woo factor I needed to win her over. I just needed to figure out a way to let her know that she was moving.

Heading inside the building, I could already tell that this was one hundred times better than the place she was currently living in. For one thing, it was secure, with the access requiring an entrance key, unlike the building she was living in, where the only security she had were the numerous locks she had on her door and the bars on her windows.

The vacant apartment was located on the fifth floor. It might be a little bit of a chore getting her stuff in the elevator, but if worse came to worse, there still were the five flights of stairs. Lou's cousin gave him the key to the apartment I was supposed to look at. I had never met the guy, but I guess he was a slumlord and had several apartment buildings that he owned. Unfortunately, his obligations were in a different place at the moment.

As Lou unlocked the door, I could smell the fresh coat of paint. The lighting in the apartment made it bright and cheery. This was a positive change from Nikki's apartment, which was dark and depressing. My only conclusion as to why she preferred the darkness was because it was her way to close herself off from the rest of the world. Stepping further inside the apartment, it had been partially furnished. The furnishings were simple, but nice. It made me wonder if the rent was going to be more since it had been newly furnished. Seeing my concern, Lou patted my shoulder and said, "It's included, bro."

"How is it that you manage to know what I'm thinking?" I asked.

"Because your face is easy to read." Lou

confessed with a small chuckle.

Smiling back at him, we walked over to the kitchen. Once again, the appliances were simple but nice. It was also pretty good sized, at least twice the size of Nikki's current kitchen, if not more. The openness may have had something to do with it, that and the floor-to-ceiling windows that brought in the sunshine.

Moving down the hallway, I noticed that there was an intercom system mounted to the wall, along with what looked to be an alarm system. Checking out the panel, I looked over to Lou and said, "This is nice. A step up from her current security."

Shaking his head, Lou stepped past me and said, "Let's check out the bedroom. I think she will be really satisfied with it."

Walking into the bedroom, I immediately knew without a doubt that this room was way bigger than the shoebox Nikki slept in, and with an ensuite bathroom, this was by far a better option for her. Looking inside, there was a shower and a tub. I could picture Nikki surrounded with bubbles with me behind her, caressing those gorgeous breasts of her.

With a half smile, Lou chucked, "Yeah, pretty great," like he knew exactly what was on my mind.

Finishing the tour of the apartment, I clarified, "So let me get this straight, the apartment and the furnishings are only $1200 a month?" I asked.

"Yup. That, plus first and last months' rent," he added.

"Tell your cousin I'll take it." I said with confidence. Even though Nikki had no clue what was in store for her, I knew without a doubt that she would love this place.

"You sure about this, Sly?" Lou asked with concern.

"Yeah, I'm sure. Once I let her know it is either

here or moving in with me, I'm pretty sure she is going to accept it," I replied.

"Okay, bro. It's all yours."

Lou handed me the keys to the apartment with a grin. I had a funny feeling he thought I lost it. If he saw the dump that Nikki was living in, I knew he would understand why I was doing this. Call me crazy, but I just couldn't wait around for something bad to happen to Nikki. Now the only thing I needed to do was convince her to forget about the fight that was scheduled to take place next Saturday. I had to find a way to let her know that I knew.

CHAPTER NINE

Nikki

When Sly called me to let me know not to make any plans, I had no idea what he was up too. I wasn't even sure if I would be up to doing anything, the way my body felt. Carly gave me a run for my money the way she was sparring with me, but when I planted my fist against her temple, I thought for sure she was gone. Watching a lifeless body laying on a sweat-riddled mat was something I never wanted to see again. If it weren't for Carlos and the debt I owed, I would never step another foot in a ring again.

Lost in my thoughts, I heard a light knock on the door. Pulling my phone from my pocket I could see it was 5:00 p.m., which could only mean that Sly was on the other side. Opening the door, there he stood, in 6'4" magnificence. Moving to the side, I allowed him in before telling him what was really on my mind. "I'm not sure what you're up too, but this doesn't change things between us. Just friends, remember."

"You will have to wait and see. Now, put this on," Sly demanded softly as he handed me a red scarf.

"I'm not putting that thing on," I cursed.

"Well, then I guess you don't get to see your surprise."

Grabbing the silk scarf from him. I place it over my eyes as I argued. "I don't know what the big deal is."

Being blindfolded and walking down three flights of stairs wasn't the easiest thing to do. For one, it left a weird feeling in my stomach and for another, I hated not being able to see where I was going. Sly must have realized how uncomfortable I was walking down the steps, because his arms came around me, lifting me into his. Even though it was much better and the queasiness in my stomach went away, it still would have been better if I could see.

The minute the cool breeze hit my face, I knew that we had made it outside. Sly set me down on the sidewalk so that he could open the door to his Jeep. Touching my head, he said, "Watch your step," before he helped me inside. Snapping the seatbelt into place, I heard the door close. Sitting back in the seat, I took a deep breath, knowing that Sly wouldn't do anything to hurt me.

As he started the engine, the radio came on with *'Can't Stop the Feeling'* by Justin Timberlake. I didn't know what it was, but somehow I felt comforted, not only by the song that was on the radio, but also by the scent of Sly's cologne that filled the small space. Maybe it was my heightened senses taking over since I couldn't see.

I still didn't have a clue where we were going. We had been traveling for what must have been half an hour. I was just about to call this little game of Sly's over when he reached over and took hold of my hand. "We are almost there, baby."

Just the sound of 'baby' rolling off his tongue made my heart beat faster. No one had ever called me that before. If it had been anyone else, I would have told them to go fuck themselves. In general, I hated pet names, and being called 'baby' or 'honey' was at the top of the list as my most hated ones.

I knew we must have reached out destination when Sly turned off the engine. I was about to remove the red scarf from my eyes when Sly gently squeezed my hand. "Not yet, baby."

I was really beginning to get annoyed at this whole game Sly was playing. Hearing the latch on the door, I waited patiently while Sly got to my side of the car. I wasn't about to step out of the Jeep. I had no idea where we were and I wasn't ready for any more surprises. As soon as Sly opened the door, I searched for the buckle of my seatbelt. The minute it was undone, Sly took hold of my arm and guided me out. When my feet hit the ground, I knew that I was standing on concrete. The noise in the background told me that we were in the city.

Grabbing my hand tightly, he led me, while I

gripped his arm with the other hand. When I heard the turn of a key, I waited until Sly tugged me forward. There was a ding sound that could have been coming from an elevator. Hearing the voices of two women, I was certain we were in a building of some sort.

"Watch your step, baby, we are getting on the elevator," Sly cautioned me.

When I was safely inside and the doors closed, I asked with curiosity, "Where are we, Sly?"

"Almost there," he answered, squeezing my hand.

Exiting the elevator, we finally stopped and Sly once again unlocked a door. As I still held on to his arm, he guided me inside and said, "You can take the blindfold off now, baby."

"Finally," I said as I pulled the scarf over my head.

Adjusting to the light, I realized we were in an apartment. I just didn't know whose. Realizing that I was still holding on to him, I quickly dropped my hand and proceeded further inside the apartment. It was very clean and I could smell the hint of paint in the air like it had just been painted. As I looked around, it was a very nice place. The first thought that came to mind was, *"Whose place was this and why were were here?"* It looked like someone lived here, but there were no personal items anywhere.

Turning toward him, I asked with concern, "Sly, whose place is this? It is definitely not yours."

"It's yours, actually," he began. "I couldn't stand worrying about you all the time in the current dump you were living in."

"My place may be a dump, but at least it's mine," I said defensively.

"Yeah, well, this is yours now. You will never have to worry about all that yelling or having to wonder if someone is going to break in," he paused, taking my hand and leading me down the hall. "See this, baby? It's a security system. All you have to do is set it before you leave and turn it off when you come back."

I did have to admit that was kind of cool. Pulling away from him, I glided my hand over the panel before heading down the hall. Pushing open one of the doors, it was a bedroom, and a big one at that. At least twice the size of my current bedroom. There was also a connecting bathroom, kind of like those fancy hotels had. Numbers began going around in my head, wondering just how much this place cost per month.

"Sly, you shouldn't have brought me here. There is no way I can afford a place like this. Not with what I make at the Happy Cow," I reminded him.

"I knew you were going to say that. I checked it out before I brought you here. The rent is only a hundred bucks more than you're paying now. With everything it has to offer, how could you not want to live here?"

"Maybe because a hundred bucks is a lot of money when you don't have it to spend," I said.

"Come on, Nikki. I know you like this place and I

know you would be a hundred times safer here. Isn't that alone worth the extra hundred bucks?"

I knew Sly was right. This place was a hundred times better than the place I was living in. It was in a nicer neighborhood too. I guessed I could look for a second job once this fight was over and I wasn't spending every free minute I had training. Maybe Erin would give me additional hours to make up the difference in the rent. Feeling defeated, yet excited about not living in fear, I walked over to Sly and gave him a kiss on the cheek. "Thank you for finding this place for me."

It was the sweetest thing that anyone had ever done for me. To have someone care about me was another thing that I didn't have. Sure, Carlos always kept an eye on me and made sure nothing happened to me, but that was only because I was his property and he had to make sure his investment was taken care of.

Slipping past Sly, I felt a pull on my arm. Our bodies collided together and our mouths met. When he reached around my neck, I felt a light pull on my hair as Sly removed the hairtie that was holding it in place. My hair fell down my back. With our lips still pressed together, Sly tilted me back long enough to place his arm around the backside of my legs and lift me into the air. He then carefully carried me over to the couch, where he gently lowered me. Straddling my body with one leg kneeling on the couch and the other on the floor, he slowly removed my t-shirt dress, breaking our connection for only a minute.

My heart was beating so fast, I thought it was going to come out of my chest. The effect Sly had on me was nothing I had ever experienced before. He had a pull on me that I could no longer fight. Placing his mouth on my covered breast, the heat from his breath seeped through the thin material of my bra, causing my nipples to harden in an instant.

Lowering the cup of my bra, his mouth was over my nipple, circling and sucking the hard bud, sending my body skyrocketing. When he moved his mouth even lower down my body, the tingling sensation within my core began to take over. Ripping his shirt off, without even undoing the buttons, my mouth was on him. His scent filled my senses in such a way, I became an uncontrollable crazy person fighting for what I needed most.

It was only after he took hold of my hands and placed them above my head that my need for him abated, only because of the calming tone of his voice. "It's okay, baby. Nice and slow."

With a tender touch, he placed his hand on my cheek before lowering his lips to mine. Our kiss was no longer rushed. It was passionate and filled with such emotion, even I could no longer deny what was really happening between us. Releasing my hands, Sly stood, looking at me with intent eyes while unzipping his own pants. I watched as he lowered them down his muscular legs and dropped them next to mine. Looking up and down his gorgeous body, his cock was erect. It was the most invitingly beautiful part of a man's anatomy that I had ever seen. Taking his place beside me, he pulled me on top of him with little to no effort. Spreading my legs so that I was straddling his hard body, he placed two fingers in his mouth and lowered them between our bodies.

My body came totally undone as he slipped his moistened finger under my lacy panties and inside my already wet pussy. I needed more than just his finger inside me, but when he added another, it took everything I had not to spill my juices on them. I leaned back, holding my body up with my hands. Sly curved his fingers, hitting me in just the right spot while his thumb was doing magical things against my clit. If he continued the way he was, I would be coating his fingers before I even felt his cock inside me. Lifting my body up slightly. I wrapped my arms around his shoulders and whispered softly, "Please take me. I need to feel you inside me,"

Just like that, he removed his fingers from my vagina. Tearing my panties from my body, Sly positioned his cock to my entrance. Slowly, I began rocking my hips back and forth, needing to feel more of him inside me. I wanted to feel all of him and not just the head of his cock at my entrance. I came down a little further, easing lower onto his shaft. Sly let me take control, allowing me to lower myself down on him at my own pace. God, he felt so good. It was so hard for me not to just let go and let him engulf me, but I knew, given his size, I needed to take things slow until my body was able to fully accept him.

Inch by inch I worked him inside, swaying my hips until he was fully seated inside. When he placed his hands on my hips, I knew that I no longer had control and that he was going to take over, giving me the pleasure my body was searching for. Thrust after thrust, his pulsating shaft pushed deeper and deeper inside. My heart was beating so fast, I needed to let go. Unable to breathe, my body shook uncontrollably, letting go of the emotional turmoil my body had been holding on to. Feeling a freedom I longed for, the gates opened and my tears spilled.

CHAPTER TEN

Sly

Lying in the dark with only the light from the moon shining through the window, I could think of nothing else but the feelings I was beginning to have for Nikki. With my body contorted in such a way no person in their right mind would be comfortable, I decided that I needed to move. It was time to sleep in a real bed. Wearing only my shirt, I lifted Nikki from the couch and carried her to the door, leaving the semi-furnished apartment. Starting tomorrow, this was going to be her new residence.

Placing her gently in the front seat of the Rubicon, I buckled her in before closing the door. The minute I got behind the wheel, her soft voice said, "Where are we going?"

Knowing that my place was closer than hers, I answered back, "My place."

Nikki adjusted her position without an argument, which was a first for her. Placing her head against the window, I looked over to her, realizing that she had barely anything on and was cuddled so tightly in her seat that she had to be freezing. Turning the dial on the dash, I adjusted the temperature so it would be warm enough for her.

Trying hard to keep my eyes on the road, and not on her gorgeous legs and the curve of her impeccable ass, I took a quick look behind my shoulder. While still trying to keep an eye on the road, I grabbed the small blanket I kept in the back seat for emergencies and carefully covered Nikki with it.

When I finally pulled into my spot in the covered parking garage, I was more than ready to get some sleep. Careful not to wake Nikki, I turned off the engine and quietly opened my door. Nikki had been huddled so tightly in a ball that I had no other choice but to whisper,

"Baby, you have to open up a little." When her arms went around my neck and she unfolded her body, I was able to lift her from the seat with ease.

Once inside my apartment, I disarmed the alarm and took Nikki to my room. It felt strange having a woman in my place. Normally I would go to their place, mostly because, if it didn't work out, at least they didn't know where I lived. Carrying Nikki to my room, I held her with one arm while trying to turn down the bed. With the covers pulled away, I gently set her on the side of the bed I never slept on, and covered her with the thick comforter that I rarely used. After she was settled, I walked to the bathroom to do my thing before I went to bed.

Snuggling in beside her, I pulled her closer to my body and gently kissed her on the cheek. Looking down at her, I said in a hushed tone, "Sleep tight, angel baby."

~****~

"Get the fuck off of me, you bastard," I heard her

scream in a heart-wrenching voice. I wasn't sure if she was talking to me or just dreaming. Pushing from the bed, I leaned over to find that her eyes were still closed, telling me that she was dreaming. *"It must have been some dream,"* I thought to myself. I didn't know if I should just let her ride it out or wake her. Taking a chance, I gave her a little nudge, hoping that she wouldn't pop me one.

When her fist came flying in my direction, I tried to duck out of the way, but I wasn't quick enough. "God, fucking shit," I hissed, knowing that if that didn't wake her, I was going to get a bucket of water.

"Mother of holy hell," she cursed back at me, holding her hand.

"God damn, girl, you gotta a mean punch," I confessed.

Nikki was looking at me like I had grown a set of horns. Placing my hand over my jaw, I tried to rub out the sting. When the expression on her face changed, I knew she realized what she had done. Pushing herself from the bed, she ran in the direction of the bathroom, closed the door, and locked it. I wasn't sure what the hell was going on, but locking herself in the bathroom was a no-go. Throwing the covers off, I swung my legs over the side of the bed and walked over to the bathroom. Knocking lightly on the door, I said, "Nikki, open the door."

"Go away, Sly." she cried, " Please just go away."

"I'm not going away until you open this door and we can talk."

I heard the click of the lock, but she never opened the door. Taking a chance, I turned the knob and pushed the door open. There she was, sitting on the toilet with her head lowered between her hands. Walking over to her, I lowered my body in front of her so I was at the same level as her. Lifting her chin so that I could see her face, I saw that she had been crying.

In a tender, but stern voice, I asked, "What's going on with you, baby? Did something happen to you to cause such a dream?"

When she opened her mouth like she was about to say something and then closed it, I knew she wasn't ready to tell me what was going on. Her head lowered again to her lap. Raising her chin again, I looked at her in a way I knew she would understand. Her mouth opened again, but this time she said, "I did something really bad."

"What?" I asked, unsure if I heard her correctly.

"It happened ten years ago." Nikki said, tears running down her face.

"What happened, Nikki?"

"Please, Sly, don't make me tell you. I just can't."

"Does this have to do with your fighting?" The minute the words left my mouth, I knew I was caught.

"You know about me fighting? How could you know... unless? Oh, my God, you've been spying on me," she cursed, pushing me away from where she was sitting. "How could you, Sly?"

I didn't even have the chance to explain, before she was out of the bathroom. "Wait, Nikki. Let me explain," I pleaded, pushing myself from the floor.

By the time I got up and out of the bathroom, I heard the slamming of the front door. Pulling my jeans on, I hurried to catch her. I knew what she was wearing and that she wasn't going to get very far unless she wanted to expose herself to the people of Manhattan. Just in case, I made a quick detour to the kitchen to grab my keys, only my keys were no longer on the counter. "Shit," I cursed, knowing Nikki swiped them before she left. Running back to my room, I went to the dresser and grabbed the keys to my bike and threw on my leather jacket that was hanging in the closet. The only thing I could hope for was that I would be able to catch up with her, either at the new apartment or her crappy old one.

~****~

When I arrived at the new apartment in Midtown,

I knew Nikki wasn't there. I should have known she wouldn't come here after finding out what I did. I'm not even sure she realized that she had the key to this place when she took the keys to the Jeep. I was in for some major sucking up with her. I'd be lucky if she ever came back to this place after what she found out.

Putting my Harley in gear, I pulled away from the curb and headed to Brownsville. This was the only other place that Nikki would be. I only prayed that she was smart enough to lock the doors on my Jeep.

Twenty minutes later I was in front of Nikki's old apartment building. Looking around, I couldn't see any sign of the Rubicon, which led me to believe that she wasn't here either. I was running out of options. I thought for sure if she wasn't at the apartment in Midtown that she would surely be here. I was beginning to worry. I was running out of places to look. Maybe she needed to let off a little steam.

When I got to the gym, I spotted the Jeep right away. *Thank God.* I had to give Nikki credit for parking it out of plain view. Placing my helmet on my bike, I walked over to the gym and opened the door. I spotted Nikki right away, abusing the punching bag and the black guy holding it steady for her. Walking in her direction, I got the feeling I wasn't welcomed by the glares I was getting from the other members. Reaching Nikki, I placed my hands in my pockets and said, "We need to talk, Nikki."

Continuing her assault on the bag she, grunted, "We have nothing to talk about."

"Please, Nikki, let me explain," I pleaded.

Stopping her movements, she looked to the guy holding the bag. "It's okay, Lewis."

The guy nodded his head before leaving us. Looking over to me, Nikki moved her head in the direction of the bench that was pushed up against the wall. Following her, I watched as she pulled the strings of her boxing glove and then put her hand under her arm to remove it. Taking a seat on the bench, I sat beside her and helped her get the other glove off her hand.

"You should have told me about your fighting," I said, handing her the other glove.

"Well, you shouldn't have spied on me," she countered.

"Nikki, why are you fighting in the first place? A boxing ring is no place for a woman," I responded, defending my actions.

"I don't have a choice, Sly. You know nothing about me. Why couldn't you just have left after that first night? It would have been so much simpler."

"Because, whether or not you want me in your life, I care about you, Nikki," I asserted, taking her trembling hand into mine.

"I don't want you to care about me. Everyone I come into contact with... dies."

"Then stop this craziness. Don't fight on Saturday." The look on her face was even more angry than when she left my apartment. "I know about the fight, Nikki. Your friend Lewis told me about it."

"Yeah, well Lewis needs to learn to keep his mouth shut."

"What is this really about, Nikki? Are you in some kind of trouble?"

"Leave it alone, Sly. Please, just leave it alone," she begged hysterically before standing and walking away.

"Nikki, what is it?"

"Leave it alone, Sly."

Before I could say anything more she was out of sight. Something was going on. She was hiding something. Whatever it was, I was going to find out. She could keep her secrets, but eventually I would find out myself.

CHAPTER ELEVEN
Nikki

The only thing I could think about was how much Sly really knew about me. He confessed that he knew about the fight, but didn't say anything about Carlos and the debt I owed him. Lewis had no right to tell him about the fight.

Closing my locker, I looked at the inside of the door where I taped a picture of my mom. She was the only person who really understood me. God, how I missed her. I kissed my index finger and swiped it along the faded picture of both of us together. I couldn't even remember when the picture was taken. I was so young. I was so happy back then. Now, I was just numb.

Grabbing my things, I left the locker room hoping

that Sly was no longer hanging around. I left Sly's keys with Lewis, knowing that he would eventually find me. I should have exited out the back door instead of out the front. Standing with his leg crossed over the other leaning against his Jeep was the one man I wished would just go away.

"We are not talking about this, Sly," I said as I walked down the sidewalk away from him.

"Did I say anything, Nikki? I was just waiting to give you ride," he replied as he began walking behind me.

Stopping in my tracks, I turned to face him. Even though he towered above me, I held my own by pulling my shoulders back and pushing to my tiptoes to gain a little bit more height. "I don't need a ride. I only live a few blocks away."

"You are not going back to that dump. Besides, your landlord has already been notified that you were moving out," he began as he brought his cell to life.

"Yup, right about now the guys should be just about done moving your stuff."

"You can't be serious. You can't do that," I hissed.

"Already done. Now are you going to get in the Jeep or am I going to have to carry you?"

I was beyond pissed at him. *Who did he think he was, controlling my life like that?* He may have won this time, but in the end it would be me that came out as the victor.

~****~

When we got to my new apartment, several men were walking inside with what looked to be some of my things. I remembered all of them, at least their big muscular bodies. As I entered the apartment, Cop and Peter were ready to grab another load. Cop was my friend Sabrina's husband and Peter was Lilly's husband. Sabrina worked with me at the Happy Cow, before she decided to work for Lilly at her art gallery, which was right across the street from the little coffee shop. I wasn't sure what happened between Brie and me, but somehow we drifted apart.

As the guys continued bringing my stuff in, I didn't realize how much I actually had until the boxes began piling up in the living area. Sly must have noticed my frustration with all these guys running in and out of the apartment.

"Guys, hold up for a minute," he said loudly so they could hear. When he got their attention, he continued. "Not sure if you remember Nikki, but this is her new place."

I waved my hand, and said, "Hi."

"Nikki,I'm not sure if you remember all the guys.. They all work at Jagged Edge Security," Sly jumped in.

One by one he introduced me to the guys. I had met them only briefly in Kierabali at Isabelle's wedding.

There was Lou Gainer, Ash Jacobs, Mike Chavez, Ryan Hyatt and his brother Josh. And of course Peter and Cop, who I already knew. All of them were as hot as could be. I almost felt like I stepped into an all-male review, aside from the fact that they were all fully clothed.

When Sly brought in the last box, most of the other guys had already left. Peter was the only one who hadn't, but he said his goodbyes when Sly came through the door. Trying to find a place to set it down, I looked around and shoved over a box so that Sly could place it in its spot. I knew that I had my work cut out for me when I looked around the room.

Plopping down in the chair that was brought over from the other apartment, I took a deep breath, wondering where I was going to start first. Hearing some noise coming from down the hall, I pushed up from the chair and headed in that direction. Glancing inside the bedroom, I saw that Sly was busy putting a bed together. It wasn't the bed that had been in my other apartment. This one was much bigger and looked a lot more expensive than what I would have been able to afford.

Matter of fact, all of the furnishings in the bedroom weren't mine, and matched the bed Sly was trying to assemble perfectly.

Walking over to where he was kneeling on the floor, I questioned him, perturbed as hell, "What the hell is all of this, Sly?"

Looking up at me with one of his super-sexy smiles, he said, "A house-warming gift."

"Looks more like a charity donation than a house-warming gift," I sputtered.

"Jesus, Nikki. Can't you accept anything from someone without being defensive about it?" he replied with an irritable tone.

"I have never taken handouts and I am not going to start now."

"Good, then you can help me put this thing together."

Kneeling on the floor beside him, I held the base of the bed frame up so that he could screw it together. I had to admit that we worked well together as long as we weren't saying nasty things to each other. It took us no time at all to finish putting the bed together. Hoisting the box spring and mattress on the king-sized bed, we both flopped down on it to check out its comfort. This bed was way nicer than the secondhand bed I bought for twenty bucks at the thrift store.

As we laid there side by side, I could feel my body begin to tingle. Sly reached over and took my hand, brushing it against his lips. Just the feel of his lips made this moment between us seem natural. Like we had been together for years rather than a few weeks. Sly rolled over on his side and began staring down at me with a serene look in his eyes like I was some heavenly angel. Sweeping his hand across my face to move away a stray hair, he lowered his lips to mine and gently kissed me. My mouth parted, needing to feel him. He softly nipped at my lower lip, causing a wave of pleasure to surge down my body. Wrapping my arms around his shoulders,

I drew him closer to me.

Soon we were at each other, unable to get enough, like a dying need. Tugging at each other's clothes like animals, our desire for each other erupted into a heated rush that neither of us had any control over. With Sly's muscular frame tilted over mine, I could feel the warmth of his breath as he inched closer to me. Kissing the top of my head, he looked at me with compassion before whispering, "This is us, Nikki. The way it's supposed to be."

I knew exactly what he was saying. This was us. I had never felt for any man the way I was feeling at this very second, and when he placed his mouth over mine in such a tender heavenly manner, I knew we were meant to be. The bad was somehow taken away by the delicate touch of his lips to mine. When he moved inside me, it was like he was confessing that he would forever protect me, keep me safe. His body covered mine as he brought me closer to him, shielding me in his warmth. Resting my head on his shoulder to cover the emotions that were having a tug-of-war with my heart, I couldn't fight the pull any more. The first tear escaped. I watched it slowly run down the sculpted muscles of Sly's back. One after another they fell, showering him with the unmistakable love I was beginning to have for him

With a shudder of pure ecstasy, my walls came down and the truth spilled as I screamed his name like he was my only savior. Feeling the grip I had on him, his barrier broke and his confession filled the room. "I'm yours, baby, please say you are mine."

~****~

There was a chill in the air as we were nestled in each other arms, keeping each other as warm as we could. It didn't matter how tightly Sly held me, I was shivering. It could have been from the cold air, or it might have been from the emotional ride I just got off of. Pulling away from me, he left me shivering even more. "I'm going to try and find something to cover us with," he whispered as he pulled away from me.

It didn't take him long to find the bedding in one of the boxes in the living room. Draping it over my body first, Sly crawled underneath the thick blanket and once again held me tight. Placing my head on his shoulder, he felt good. As hard as his chest was, I was enveloped with comfort. I knew I would sleep like a baby, only that didn't happen. I could only think about the fight I was about to enter and the fact that I hadn't told Sly anything about my past. I wasn't sure what was going to happen between us, but I knew that if I wanted to continue keeping him in my life, I needed to let him know about my past.

Lifting my head, thinking it was now or never, I watched him as he slept. I just couldn't pull my eyes away from how beautiful he really was. Every curve of his face was perfect. Even the small scar above his right eye made him more handsome. Lifting my hand to his face, I began tracing the fullness of his lips with my finger. My touch was light enough so that I knew he wouldn't wake. Moving from his lip, I traced the bridge of his nose. There was a small bump, but unnoticeable by just looking at him. It was perfect.

Placing my hand back underneath my head, I

rested my head on his chest. I could feel and hear every beat of his heart. It was only after he said, "Good night, baby," that I knew he felt every touch I placed on his face. Kissing his chest lightly, I closed my eyes and fell into a blissful sleep.

CHAPTER TWELVE
Nikki

When morning came, I didn't want to move. Sly was no longer by my side and the scent of coffee brewing filled the air. I knew he was up and getting ready for the day. Stretching my body, I pulled the covers up over my body to stay warm. I wasn't sure what was going on with me, but I couldn't get warm enough. Nixing the idea of staying in bed, I threw off the covers and swung my legs over the side of the massive bed.

The minute I sat up, I felt crummy. It wasn't the sore kind of crummy I usually felt after my training, it was more like the achy, icky feeling, like when I was getting sick. Pushing from the bed, I tried to make it to the bathroom. The feeling I had in my stomach told me that I was about to lose whatever was inside. I hadn't eaten much yesterday, so I knew it couldn't be much.

As I stood, I felt weird, like my legs were about to give out on me. Before I could catch myself, I went down. It wasn't one of those graceful collapses you see on TV, this was a hard earth-shattering thud that I was sure everyone in the building heard. Apparently, even Sly heard it, because he was at my side in seconds.

"Nikki! What happened? Are you okay?" he asked, concerned as he knelt beside me.

"I need to get to the bathroom. Quick!" I mumbled, barely able to talk as the bile in my throat began to make its appearance.

Just as Sly lifted me from the hard floor, I couldn't hold it any longer. My stomach had its own agenda as it churned. The contents ended up half on Sly and half on the floor in small puddles as it continued to come up my throat. I don't ever remembering being this sick before.

Looking over at Sly's chest, which was covered in puke, I said, "I'm so sorry."

"Let's get cleaned up," he suggested as he kissed the top of my head. "Jesus Christ, baby, you're burning up."

~****~

The last thing I remembered was being held by Sly as he tried to wash me in the shower. It took me a moment to realize where I was. One thing I knew for sure was that I still felt like shit. Lifting my head from the pillow, it dawned on me that Sly must have made the bed. Trying hard to push myself in a sitting position, I looked around the room and noticed that most of my things had been unpacked as well.

I wasn't sure how long I was out, but it was obvious it wasn't a couple of minutes. Pushing from the bed, I slowly walked to the door and into the hall. I could hear the soft sound of 'Old Republic' coming from the living area. As I turned the corner, I couldn't believe what I saw. All of the boxes that were piled in the living room earlier were now gone. I should have been angry with Sly for getting into all of my personal stuff, but I wasn't. More than anything, I was glad I didn't have to unpack the boxes myself.

Standing in the nicely decorated living room, I didn't see Sly anywhere. Even though the music was playing, he wasn't in the apartment. I couldn't understand why he would up and leave without saying anything. Spotting my cell phone on the small table in front of the couch, I made an effort to get to it so I could call him and find out where he was. Just as I was bringing up his number, the front door opened.

"Hey, you're awake," I heard him say behind me.

"Yeah," I answered softly as I turned toward him.

"I got you something to eat. You have to be hungry after sleeping for two days straight," he said.

"Wait, what day is it?" I asked, confused by his remark.

"It's Thursday."

"Thursday?" I questioned in disbelief.

I lost two days. Two days that I should have been training instead sleeping. "I need to get to the gym," I cursed frantically, unaware that I was putting on my tennis shoes while still in my pajamas.

"Hold on, Nikki. You need to get better first. You still don't look very good. At least try and eat something first," Sly demanded.

Knowing that Sly was right, I sat back down on the couch and took in a deep breath. I still wasn't back to my old self, which was not normal for me. The lightheadedness started again. I blamed it on the lack of food in my stomach, but somehow I knew it was because I wasn't a hundred percent yet.

Stretching out on the couch and pulling the throw blanket over my body, I watched as Sly began preparing me something to eat. Even though I wasn't much of a cook, but always managed to eat healthy, it was strange watching Sly in the kitchen, moving around like he spent most of his time there.

As weird as I thought it was, when he brought me what he had fixed, I was thoroughly amazed. Sly prepared me a bowl of oatmeal with blueberries sprinkled on the top and two slices of buttered toast. I didn't even think I owned a toaster, unless he went out and purchased one for me. Setting my meal on the small table, he sat beside me and helped me to sit up. Taking the bowl of oatmeal from the table, he dipped the spoon inside, grabbing two plump blueberries, and held the spoon to my mouth. I wasn't much of an oatmeal eater, but this was by far the best I had ever tasted. Him feeding me might have had something to do with it as well.

After I finished what I could of Sly's amazing meal, he assisted me to the bathroom. Not that he really needed to, but with his lips stuck to mine, there really wasn't any other option. Setting me on the toilet, he began filling the tub full of water. This would be the first bath I had taken in my new apartment. As the water flowed in the large tub, Sly poured in some soothing bubble bath that had the scent of lilies and vanilla. Ridding myself of my clothes, Sly held my hand to steady me as I stepped into the heavenly scented water.

While I was relaxing in the mound of white lather, Sly decided to finish cleaning up the dishes in the kitchen. I missed his company, but it was nice to relax for a moment with nothing but silence. Shutting my eyes, I submersed my body further down inside the tub and leaned my head against the rim. *"Yep, I could definitely get used to this."*

I must have dozed off for a minute or two, because my body jerked at the loud voices that were coming from outside the door. I recognized the one voice as Sly's, but I had no idea whose the other one was. Feeling it was time to go investigate. I placed my hands on the edge of the tub and pushed myself out of the water.

Once I was dried off, I put on the comfortable clothes that Sly must have laid out for me, and headed in the direction of the arguing men I heard just moments ago. When I finally got to the living area, the arguing had stopped and only Sly was there. He was looking out the window with his arm stretched out and his hand against the window. I could tell he was tense. Whoever he was having it out with must have had an impact on his mood.

Quietly I walked up beside him and placed my hand on his shoulder. "Who were you fighting with a moment ago?" I asked.

"Someone that shouldn't have been here," he answered defensively.

I stood still and I watched him head to the couch to grab his coat. Slipping it on, he walked back over to where I stood stunned and kissed me lightly on the forehead. "Are you going to be okay for a while? There's something I need to take care of."

"Where are you going?" I asked.

"To the shop."

I didn't even know what that meant. Moving past me, he opened the front door, leaving me alone. No matter how badly I wanted to follow him to find out what was really going on with him, I knew I had more important things to do.

~****~

Changing into my jeans and a t-shirt, I slipped on my gray hoodie and set the alarm to the apartment. Sly had set the security system up for me and he thought it would be better to pick a code that we both would remember. It was pretty simple, really, 'home.' I pressed 4663 on the pad and waited for it to engage before I opened the door.

It felt good to be back in the gym. Carly was already in the ring practicing her footwork with one of the trainers. She also was scheduled to fight on Saturday.

The only difference between me and her was that she chose to be in the ring, whereas I was forced. I never told her why I became an MMA fighter. As far as she knew, I got my kicks beating the shit out of women.

Standing on the edge of the ring holding onto the middle rope, I watched Carly work the ring. When she spotted me, she gave her trainer a nod and headed my way. Pulling her mouthpiece out, she squatted to my level and looked at me with concern. "Hey, Nik. Where have you been? You know the fight is in two days."

"Yeah. I must have caught the flu or something. Been pretty sick," I confessed.

"Bummer. Are you going to be okay to fight on Saturday? I heard that Black Jewel chick has been training crazy hard. There was even a live stream of her posted. She looks pretty good, Nik," Carly warned.

"Yeah, I'll be ready."

I hadn't seen the video that Carly was talking

about and I wasn't about to psych myself out by watching it. Pushing from the rope, I knew I had better get training or Black Jewel was going to slaughter me.

CHAPTER THIRTEEN

Sly

"Fuck, fuck, fuck," I thought to myself as I headed out of Nikki's apartment building. Of all things, why the hell did my father have to show up at her apartment? And how the fucking hell did he know where to find me? The only blessing was, Nikki was still in the tub when we finished our little discussion. The last thing I needed was for her to question me about who he was or what he did for a living.

I couldn't believe what he was telling me, either. There was no way that Angelo Conti had a stake in the fight on Saturday and was willing to pay Nikki a sizable amount of money for throwing the fight. How could I even tell her that my dad worked for the biggest Mafia family in New York? I needed to get my head around this. I had a funny feeling that this fight might be more than just a fight between two women, and my dad made that abundantly clear before he left. Maybe with a little digging I would be able to find out the story behind Nikki's choice of careers. But most importantly, I needed to find out what she wasn't telling me.

Parking my Jeep behind Peter's Camaro, I got out and started in the direction of the shop when I saw Mike and Ash coming out. "Hey, guys, where you headed? " I asked.

"Some lady on Park Avenue is having trouble with her security system. She's afraid to go inside her apartment. Something about hearing weird noises," Ash explained.

"Well, good luck," I said with a chuckle. I knew exactly the lady they were referring to. I was there about a month ago for the same reason. I think more than anything she was just a lonely woman who was looking for someone to keep her company for a while. When I suggested she get a dog, she said she would, but apparently that hadn't happened yet.

Opening the door, I looked over at the pool table where Hawk and I used to play. I really missed having him around, but I knew that he was happy in Kierabali with Isabelle. Hopefully they would find the time to come back here.

Peter was back in the conference room. I could see him working on his laptop through the glass windows. Finishing with my 'Hellos' to the other guys, I headed that way. Tapping lightly on the door to get his attention, I entered and closed the door behind me. Peter looked up at me, probably wondering what was on my mind.

Taking a seat directly across from him, I asked him openly, "I need your help. I think Nikki might be in trouble."

The minute he closed the lid on his laptop, I knew

I had his attention. "What's going on, Sly? Don't leave anything out."

After spending about half an hour explaining to Peter everything I knew about Nikki, including the information about my father, I knew Peter was trying to sort this shit out. By the look on his face, I knew I was fucked. I only hoped that he would be able to help me with the situation that could possibly put the only woman I gave a shit about in harm's way.

"The first thing we need to do, Sly, is a thorough background check on Nikki. There must be something in her past that will let us know how to handle this fight on Saturday and what to expect," Peter suggested.

"What do you need from me? Nikki trusts me, so I'm pretty sure I can get what you need. I've already gone through all her stuff when I unpacked it. There wasn't anything among her things that said anything about her or her past. It was like she had none," I confessed.

"Well, there should be a birth record for her and

that will at least tell us about her parents. Maybe if we could find them, we could put together a past for her, and find out what she's hiding."

"I don't know what you'll find, Peter. One thing I do know is that her parents are no longer living. Not sure how they died, but Nikki only said that they died when she was young."

"Well, then we will start there. There has to some sort of death record on them. I'll see what I can find out when I run the check. In the meantime, stay close to her." Peter ordered.

Pushing from the long table, I gave him a nod and headed towards the door. Before I opened it, there was another thing that I remembered. "Peter, were there any hits on the partial plate I gave you?"

"Not yet, bro."

"I think that is going to be our ticket to find the truth about Nikki's past. Whoever was inside the SUV was someone with power. I have a funny feeling that whoever he is, he may be holding something over her," I pointed out before leaving the room.

The ride back to my place was long and exhausting. I needed a shower and get back to Nikki's place to see if there was anything else I could find. One thing I knew for sure. It wouldn't hurt to check out her locker at the gym. Sometimes a person's most valued possession could be found there.

~****~

When I got to Nikki's place, the alarm had been set, but there was no sign of her. I punched in the code and then went to her room to see if maybe she was sleeping. Opening the door, I looked inside to find that the bed was still unmade, but she wasn't in it. She could only be at one other place, the gym. Setting the alarm, I closed the door and made sure it was locked. I couldn't believe Nikki would be there after feeling so sick the past couple of days.

Jumping back in my Jeep, I took the fastest route to the gym. I could have had a dozen tickets, by the way I was weaving in and out of traffic and exceeding the speed limit on more than one occasion. Reaching the gym in record time, I was disappointed to find that there were no lights on. I was beginning to worry when a figure walked out of the gym door. I waited in the Jeep for a moment to see if I could tell who it was. I would know that body anywhere. Turning off the engine, I got out and jogged across the street to where Nikki was.

"Nikki, wait," I yelled, so she would at least slow down so I could catch up to her.

The minute she turned towards me, I knew something was wrong. I hurried to her side while she waited for me. Her face was hidden by the hood of her jacket, so I lifted her chin. I could see that something was definitely wrong. I lowered the hood to find the beautiful face that I loved so much was busted up pretty badly. Her lip was swollen with a cut along the bottom and there was bruising under her left eye, barely open enough for her to see.

"My God, baby, what happened to you?" I asked, ready to kill the person who did this to her.

"It's nothing, Sly," she cried.

"Bullshit if it's nothing. Who did this, Nikki?" I demanded she tell me.

"Please, Sly. Just leave it alone. I'm begging you," she pleaded.

"I'm not going to leave this alone, Nikki. Not this time. Who did this to you?" I asked again.

"Not here, Sly. I'll tell you, but not here."

The way she looked at me, she was downright scared. It was only her and I standing outside the gym, or so I thought. The minute a set of headlights came on, I knew we weren't alone. What I didn't count on was the pair of headlights to come right at us. Pushing Nikki out of the way was the only thing that kept her from getting hit. I looked over to her briefly to make sure she was okay before darkness hit.

CHAPTER FOURTEEN
Nikki

The people that were walking back and forth in front of me were driving me crazy. I don't know how long I sat beneath the bright fluorescent lights, but my lip was throbbing and the ability to see out of my left eye was nearly impossible. I still hadn't heard anything on Sly. *"Why did he have to push me?"* I said to myself, wondering where he was at. My patience finally ran out and I couldn't spend one more minute here without knowing anything.

Pushing from the hard bed in the Emergency room, I pulled open the curtain and walked over to where several people dressed in blue scrubs were standing at the nurse's station.

Squeezing between them, I asked, agitated, "Can anyone tell me what's going on with Sylvester Capelli?"

They way they all looked at me, they were probably pissed that I interrupted their little gathering. What was it with these people? Didn't saving lives mean more than having a gossip session?

Seeing my agitated look, a woman behind the desk finally began typing on her computer. With an irritated look, she replied, "Mr. Capelli is still being examined. As soon as the doctor has any information, he will let you know."

With a huff, I walked back over to the room they left me in and resumed holding the ice pack over my eye. Leaning back on the bed, I waited some more. When the curtain was flung open, the tall man that had checked me out earlier appeared.

"You are a very lucky young lady," he pointed out, looking at my chart. "The CT scan came back showing no trauma to your brain. Had the blow to your face been a few inches higher, you might not be sitting here right now. Would you please tell me what happened?"

"Not really, Doc. But I would like to know how my friend is doing. Nobody seems to know," I said rudely

"If you're referring to Mr. Capelli, he is in good hands. He has a lot of scrapes and bruising, but he should be fine. We are going to keep him here overnight for observation," the doctor responded as his brow curved upward..

"Can I see him?" I asked.

"Yes. He should be in his room now."

~****~

When I got to Sly's room, his eyes were closed and he looked to be resting. Seeing a chair next to his bed, I scooted it closer to him. The doctor was right. His face was pretty scraped up and so were his chest and arms. I was almost tempted to check out the rest of him, but I was afraid I would get caught sneaking a look under the covers. Right then a nurse walked in, pushing away my naughty thoughts.

As she checked his fluids, she kept looking over at me like I should have been the one laying in that bed. We were quite the pair. Appeasing her curiosity, I finally said, "Thought I would give bungee jumping a try."

The way she looked at me, I was pretty sure she thought I was full of shit. Turning before she left, she said bluntly, "You should put ice on that eye."

Sly must have heard her comment, because his eyes slowly opened. Standing, I leaned over the bed so I could get a better look at him. Even with his scrapes and bruises, he was still gorgeous. Taking his hand in mine, I softly said, "That was really stupid not moving out of the way."

"Yeah, well, I was kind of saving someone else,"

he grunted. "Are you going to tell me now who hit you?"

"I'm not sure I can, Sly. It is really complicated and..."

"Stop, Nikki. I don't care what it is. All I know is that I care about you and whatever it is, it won't change how I feel about you."

Taking a seat on the chair, I placed my hands in my lap and took a deep breath. I wasn't sure exactly how much I was going to tell Sly, but I knew I couldn't keep it from him any longer. I hoped he wouldn't feel differently about me once I told him the truth, like he said. "Okay, but before you say anything, let me finish what I have to say."

Sly propped his body up on one elbow with a painful groan. "Like I said, Nikki, it won't change the way I feel about you."

"I'm not sure where to begin."

"The beginning would be good," Sly replied.

"Okay, Everything started when I was thirteen, the fighting, hating my father, losing my mom. I'm not even sure how she died. One day she was there and the next she was gone."

"Go on," Sly urged

With my hands in my lap, I began picking at the skin around my index finger. "My dad was in a lot of trouble, I remember my mom and him always arguing about what he did for a living," I paused for a moment before I continued. "When a man I didn't know showed up at the door claiming to be my uncle, I knew something bad had happened. He didn't look like any uncle I ever knew. He ordered me to get my things and go with him. I kept asking him where my mom and dad were, but he wouldn't tell me. With no other choice, I left with him."

Explaining things about my past was a lot harder than I thought it would be. I didn't know if it was because it was Sly I was telling or if it was the bad memories being stirred up. Standing from the chair, I headed over to the window. Somehow it eased my mind knowing that Sly couldn't look at me as I told him the truth about my past.

"I was told that my mom got shot in a parking lot of a grocery store while she was unloading groceries into her car. They never found the man who shot her, but I was pretty sure that my dad working for Carlos Giordano had something to do with it."

"Wait a minute. You know Carlos Giordano?" Sly asked, confused.

"Yeah," I began to chuckle. "He was my long-lost uncle."

"Nikki," Sly called out before I interrupted him.

"Sly, please let me finish before I can't," I pleaded, looking over at him leaning over the side of the bed so he could see me.

Sly rested his body back on the bed and I continued to look out the window. I acted like I was looking out over the city, but I saw nothing. All I could think about was how messed up my childhood really was. "The day that Carlos took me from my home was the day my life changed forever. He told me that I was going to be the one to make up for my dad's stupidity and that he owned me until he was fully paid. That was when he introduced me to fighting. It was his passion. He organized an illegal fighting ring. Everyone who was anyone was involved. That's why he came after me at the gym. He was angry that I hadn't been training like I should have been. Thought he could find out how ready I really was, so he put one of his guys on me." I let out a small chuckle before continuing. "At least I gave him a run for his money and got a few good punches in before he knocked me out."

"You can't fight on Saturday, Nikki. This whole thing is messed up." Sly confessed.

"I have to. Don't you understand? If I don't my life could be in danger and so could yours."

162

"My life won't matter if you're dead, Nikki," Sly admitted.

"Yeah, well, fighting is a better alternative." I needed to get out of here for a while so I could clear my head.

"Wait, where are you going?" Sly asked.

"I need to get some training in. I'll stop by and check on you later."

Before Sly had a chance to say any more I left his room. I wanted so badly to feel his lips pressed to mine, but if I kissed him goodbye, I would break down and he would see how scared I really was. All my life I was able to hide my insecurities, but with Sly, the more time we spent together the harder it was hiding how truly scared I was.

~****~

As I punched the speed bag, I kept thinking about what the doctor said about the blow to my face being so close to ending my life. In a way, it would have solved all my problems. The harder I hit the bag, the madder I got at my dad for getting me into this predicament in the first place. If he was here, I would be punching him instead of this damn bag. I didn't know the whole story behind how much he actually owed Carlos, but Carlos made it very clear that my dad stole from him and now I needed to pay for his debt. I was pretty sure I had paid for that debt ten times over.

Just as I was about to move on to the punching bag, the door to the gym opened and speak of the devil, Carlos and two of his goons walked in like they owned the place. As they headed my way, I tried to ignore them as I began punching the bag.

"Glad to see that you haven't lost your ability to follow orders," Carlos said, sarcastically.

"What do you want, Carlos?" I asked as I continued to punch the bag.

"Just wanted to remind you how important it is that you win the fight Saturday. Wouldn't want anything bad to happen to you."

"Don't worry. I'll win. I can't wait for the day when I'm done with you." I seethed, looking over at his men standing behind him, one of which I left my mark on.

"Good, I'm glad were are on the same page," he paused. "It would be best for you to concentrate on winning the fight instead of dreaming about what is never going to happen. I will never be done with you, Nikki."

I could have killed him. Deep down I already knew he was never going to let me go even if the debt was fully paid. I was his money tree and as long as I was able to bring in the green, he would continue to use me. I wanted more than anything to be done with this. The fighting, Carlos, and this town.

CHAPTER FIFTEEN

Sly

When Nikki left my room, I knew I should have told her about Carlos Giordano and the rivalry he had with Angelo Conti. I just wasn't sure how to explain to her that they could have been the reason behind her mom's and ultimately her dad's death. I had to get out of here. I had this horrible feeling in my gut that something bad was going to happen to Nikki and I needed to get to her as fast as possible.

Pulling the IV from my arm and taking the monitor off of my finger, I threw the covers off my body and went to the small closet where I knew my clothes would be. I dressed as quickly as possible, hoping the nurse taking care of me wouldn't stop me from going where I needed to be.

Getting out of the hospital was the easy part. Getting to Nikki without a ride was going to be a little bit harder. My only other option was to call someone.

"Lou, I need you to come get me at St. Mary's Hospital." I demanded.

"What are you doing at the hospital, Sly? Did something happen?" Lou asked, concerned.

"I'll explain it when you get here."

Hanging up, I stayed out of sight in case some of the hospital staff came looking for me. I'm pretty sure they wouldn't, but I wasn't going to take any chances. Walking around to the side of the building, where I would still able to spot Lou's Tundra, the pain of my bruised ribs started kicking in. The pain medication they gave me must have been wearing off.

The minute Lou pulled up, I hurried over to his truck and got in. I wasn't aware of how high his truck actually was until I tried to get in. The strain on my ribs was almost more than I could handle. By the sound of my grunt and the look on Lou's face. I needed to do some explaining.

~****~

When we got to my place, Lou knew everything, except the part about who my father's current employer was. None of the guys knew about that. There was no way I was going to get them involved in the problems I had with my dad. The less they knew, the better.

All I knew was that I needed to come up with a game plan. I had less than two days to figure out what to do. One thing I did know was that the partial plate I got belonged to Carlos Giordano, according to Peter. This bit of information I kept from the officer that questioned me before I was brought to my room. Even though I wasn't one hundred percent sure who tried to eliminate me, I could pick out that SUV anywhere.

Lou waited while I took a quick shower and changed my clothes, I would have preferred facing Nikki alone, but without my Jeep, I needed a ride. Hopefully it was still in one piece when we got there. Brownsville wasn't the best place to leave a vehicle unattended, especially when that vehicle was new. When I asked Lou to take me to the gym, at first he suggested I call a cab, but then he decided that I might need more than a ride once we got there.

When Lou pulled up in front of the gym, the girl that had been fighting with Nikki a few days ago was leaving. I wasn't sure where she was headed, but my main focus was finding Nikki. Opening the door to the truck, I grunted as I lowered myself to the sidewalk. Looking over to Lou, I said, in agony. "You wait here. I am going to check inside to see if Nikki is here."

"The hell I am. If anything happens in there, you aren't in the best shape to ward off any trouble." Lou argued.

Entering the gym, I spotted Lewis and walked up

to him. Tapping him on the shoulder, I asked with no restraint, "Nikki here?"

He tilted his head pointing to the locker rooms. Nodding at him with thanks, we headed in that direction. Several men exited the men's locker room while there were no women coming out of the women's. I didn't see any other women in the gym, so I felt pretty confident that no one else would be inside the woman's locker room but Nikki, so I opened the door and entered.

Looking down each row of lockers, I finally saw Nikki. She was sitting on the bench holding what looked to be a picture in her hand. I don't think she heard me come in and she definitely didn't hear the sound of my boots on the tile floor as I approached her. Taking a seat next to her, I took her hand and pulled the picture from her grip. Holding the picture in my hand, it wasn't hard to figure out that the little girl was her and the woman next to her must have been her mom. The photo was so faded that I knew Nikki had been holding on to it for a long time. It was probably the only thing she had left of her mom.

Handing it back to her, I pulled her to my side. "We need to talk about Saturday, Nikki," I admitted.

"What's there to talk about, Sly?" she asked in a hushed tone.

"There is something you need to know. The SUV that hit me belongs to Carlos Giordano. The plate number I got was linked back to him…" I ran my hand through my hair before I continued. This was going to be the hardest thing to tell her, but I knew I needed to let her know. "This fight on Saturday may be more than a fight."

"What are you talking about, Sly?" she questioned as she turned to me.

"I haven't been exactly honest with you, Nikki. There's something you need to know about my family." Taking her hand, I rubbed it gently between my thumb and fingers "My father works for Angelo Conti," I confessed.

"What does this have to do with the fight?"

"Angelo is just like Carlos Giordano. Their families have been fighting one another for years. Not like the Hatfields and the McCoys kind of fighting either. They would take out their own family just to show who had more control."

"You aren't making any sense, Sly," she admitted, confused.

"My dad approached me with a proposition from Angelo. He wants you to throw the fight. He even suggested that there might be a little something in it for you if you did."

"I can't do that. It would be like writing my own death sentence. Carlos made it perfectly clear that I was to win that fight, and if I didn't.... Well, let's just say, it would be the end of me." Nikki stated, shaking her head back and forth.

"Somehow we need to figure out how to prevent

this fight from happening. And then we need to figure out how to get you away from this shit. Forever." Lifting Nikki's chin, I could tell that she was really worried about what was going to happen. Placing a light kiss on her lips, I whispered, "We will figure this out, baby."

When her body pushed into mine, I knew she trusted me to fix this mess. There had to be a way to stop the fight without letting Carlos or Angelo know what was going on. Maybe getting in touch with the guys and putting our heads together would bring a solution,

~****~

On the drive home, the air between Nikki and I was so thick you could have cut it with a knife. That was about the only thing you could cut, because the conversation was next to none. I knew she was worried about what was going to happen on Saturday night. It was supposed to be the fight of all fights. I could only imagine how much money was at stake. It had to be in the hundreds of thousands. Maybe in the millions.

Backing into my parking spot, we sat in silence for a few moments after I turned off the engine. It was like we were so preoccupied with our own thoughts that everything around us went unnoticed. So unnoticed that I didn't see the guy approaching the Jeep wearing nothing but black until it was too late. When he pulled out a gun and aimed it at Nikki, my only reaction was to grab her head and pull her towards me. Shot after shot, the bullets hit the Jeep, some hitting the windshield and hood while the others missed us completely.

With both of us ducking down as far as we could, I knew that soon he would be out of ammunition. After a few moments when there was no more gunfire, I raised my head to find that the guy was gone. Realizing that Nikki wasn't moving other than her hands shaking as she held them to her head, I took hold of them. "Nikki." I repeated her name several times with no response. Worried, I pulled her over the dash and into my lap.

Her body was shaking so uncontrollably, all I could do was hold her tightly and hope that she would come out of it. Once again, I spoke her name, but this time I whispered it in her ear. "Baby, I'm right here. Shh... it's okay. It will be okay."

Rocking her back and forth like my mom used to do to me whenever I got scared, I was finally able to calm her enough that she lifted her head to look at me. Without a word, she placed her lips on mine and kissed me. I could feel her tears touch my cheek as she pressed harder against me like I was going away for a long time. I knew she needed this. I needed it too. We were like two hearts trying to come together as one. I loved this woman and I was never going to let anything happen to her again.

Surveying the damage, glass was everywhere. On us, on the seat, on the dash. I was pretty sure the hit on us had something to do with Carlos Giordano. Lifting Nikki out of the jeep, I carried her to my apartment. Once she was settled on the couch, I got in touch with Peter to let him know what happened. He suggested that I take Nikki somewhere safe and stay with her. Carlos Giordano had connections and staying here wasn't an option anymore. Staying at Nikki's place was also a definite no.

While Peter was working on a way to stop the fight on Saturday, I was working on finding a safe place that Nikki and I could go. The best thing would be to find a place out of New York City, but first I needed to find a new ride. Finishing my call with Peter, I walked over to where Nikki was curled up on the couch.

Rubbing her back, I said softly, "Baby, we need to go. If Carlos had something to do with this, they might come back. I need to take you somewhere safe. Do you think you can get up?"

Her eyes were red from crying, at least one of them was. The other was so swollen that it made me want to kill Carlos for doing this to her. As she looked up at me she unfolded her body and uttered, "I'm so scared, Sly."

I knew she was scared. As tough as she pretended to be, there was a sweet defenseless woman hiding under a coat of armor. "It's okay, baby. We are going to get through this. For now we need to go."

When we got to the parking garage, Peter and Lou were waiting for us. As we walked over to them, Peter placed his hand on my shoulder and gave it a gentle squeeze. "The shooter really did a number on your Rubicon, bro."

"No shit. Luckily, it was only the Jeep and not us." I hissed.

"Here," Peter said as he handed me the keys to his Camaro. "She's all gassed up and ready to go. The key to the safe house is on there as well."

"Thanks, Peter, I'll take good care of her."

"Give me your cell phones," Peter requested as I looked at him, confused.

"What the heck for?' I asked.

"I don't want to take any chances that Carlos Giordano might be able to find you. Use these instead," he demanded, handing me a burner phone that couldn't be tracked.

"You always think of everything, bro. Glad you have my back." I admitted.

Climbing in Peter's car, I put the car into reverse and headed out of the garage. With the address Peter gave me, we were on our way to a place I knew would be safe for Nikki. I was pretty sure it was Carlos behind the shooting. Who knows what his game was? I wasn't going to stick around and find out and I wasn't taking any chances with Nikki's safety.

CHAPTER SIXTEEN

Nikki

The minute Sly pulled the seatbelt over my shoulder, reality finally set in. I couldn't believe that this was my life. Running from the one man who basically raised me and yet who I hated more than my own father. I had seen with my own eyes and had felt his wrath more than once. The fact that I would never be able to have a child of my own was evidence of that.

I would never forget the day that Carlos felt I needed to know what it meant to be a fighter. It didn't matter that I was only a child, fifteen, to be exact. I had fought my first real fight and lost. Carlos placed a lot of money on that fight on the odds that I would win. It didn't matter that the girl I was fighting against was two years older than me and at least fifty pounds heavier. I would never forget the look in her eyes. There was hate in them. Like she was ready to take out anything that got in her way, namely me.

The whole fight lasted only a few minutes and was a complete blur as each punch she landed to my head and gut pushed me that much closer to death. When the final punch landed and I fell down on the sweat-drenched mat, all I could hear was the crowd cheering, at least until everything went silent. I wish she would have killed me that day, because what happened a week later was much worse.

Carlos thought that I needed to know what it meant to be in a real fight. He said it was his way of conditioning me for the fight that was to take place the next week, only I never made that fight. The guy Carlos had chosen to show me the facts of fighting could have sat on me and I would have been out. But instead he gave me what Carlos wanted him to. Punch after punch he kept at it, knowing that I could barely stand. It didn't matter. If

A.L. Long

I was about to fall, he grabbed me by the hair to keep me upright. I knew I must have passed out at least two times. Then it was over. There was nothing left. The last thing I heard was Carlos telling him to stop. Carlos leaned over my body, his breath smelling like a cigar. "Not a word."

That was the last time I lost a fight. I knew that if I was ever going to get out from under my dad's debt, I needed to win. I had never worked so hard in my life. It didn't matter that my knuckles were swollen and bleeding. It made me work that much harder. I had no other future but to be a fighter, and I was going to be the best.

~****~

The place that Sly was given directions too wasn't that bad. It was in a secluded area in a small town about a hundred and fifty miles from New York City. Sly stopped the car in front of the tiny house and turned off the engine. Getting out, he rounded the car to my side and assisted me out. As I looked up at the tiny house, he said sarcastically, "Home Sweet Home."

181

I would have laughed at the analogy, but he was right, because I knew this was going to be our home for a while. There weren't any bags to unload from the car, so we both headed to the door. Peter thought it best to just leave without taking anything with us. He said that everything we would need would be there for us once we arrived. Unlocking the door, Sly pushed it open and stepped inside first to scan the area. Taking hold of my hand, he led me inside.

The house actually looked better on the inside than on the outside. The furniture looked to be fairly new. It was decorated very nicely as well. As I went to the kitchen, Sly went to check out the rest of the house. Just like Peter said, everything we needed was already here, with the fridge fully stocked and the cupboards as well.

Walking back to where Sly headed, I found him in the bedroom that was furnished with a dresser and a queen-sized bed. He was sitting on the bed with his head in his hands. As unbelievable as it was to swallow what happened, I knew that he was affected by what happened as much as me. Sitting next to him, I placed my head on his shoulder and wrapped my arms around him. It felt so much better when I was holding him. It was like he was my security blanket, protecting me from everything bad. Only he couldn't. He was just as much a part of this as I was. We needed each other more than ever.

Lifting his head, he turned toward me as I lifted my head from his body. The way he looked at me told me everything because I was giving him the exact same look. Moving closer, I touched my lips to his. The kiss wasn't hurried, it was just sweet and genuine and took my breath away. The affection between us was so real that it made my heart hurt. Turning towards him, I stood, lifting my leg and placing it on the other side of his body so that I was sitting across his lap. His hands caressed my back for a second before he lifted my shirt over my head. I had to catch my breath, only because I needed to tame down the rapid beating of my heart. The way he touched me sent a radiating sensation down my body all the way to my core.

Sly lifted me from his lap only to spin my body so that he could place it on the bed. Carefully lowering me down, he continued kissing me as I tried desperately to feel more of him. Tugging at his shirt to get it off, Sly lifted his body and finished what I had started by pulling his shirt the rest of the way off. When his chiseled body appeared, I could only lick my lips in delight that this for now, this moment, was mine for the taking. Placing my hands on his chest, I worked them down his muscled abs to his waist. I unbuttoned his jeans and then pulled down the zipper. I could see that the need to take me was having an effect on him as well, as his boxers struggled to keep his impressive cock tucked inside.

Gliding my index finger between the waistband of his boxers and his skin, I watched with desperation as his impressive cock appeared. Taking hold of the velvety rod, I slowly moved my hand up and down the hard length. The wetness pooled between my legs, making my panties soaked with desire for him. Placing his hand over mine, Sly moved it away and tugged on my knit top. Within seconds, my top was off and his soft lips brushed against the material of my bra, making my heart beat with rapture. Giving me one of his devilish looks, he undid the front clasp of my bra, exposing my taut buds. Caressing my breast while rolling my nipple between his finger, Sly bowed his head and brushed his lips against the sensitive peak. His tongue softly teased my nipple until he finally kissed and sucked the hard peak. The mere touch of his lips on my body caused my back to rise off the bed in hopes that I could feel more of what he was giving me.

Gripping my waist lightly with his hands, he lifted my hips and in one tug, my yoga pants and underwear were down my legs and on the floor. With his body pressed so close to mine, I knew he could feel just how wet he made me. His hand danced across my skin, finding its way to my slick folds. Dipping a finger inside my soaked channel, his moan of approval filled the small room. A burst of pleasure hit my body like a tidal wave, sending my body along with it.

"God, baby, do you know how sexy you look when you come?" he sighed between each light kiss he placed on my stomach, my nipples, my neck, until his mouth captured mine in a heated kiss that sent me over once again.

It was the most sensual thing I had ever felt. To taste my own juices on his tongue as it lapped with mine. I was so close to releasing again that I couldn't do it without him inside me. "Please, Sly, I need to feel you inside me," I pleaded as he continued his assault on my mouth.

Lifting his head, he rose above me with his knees between mine. Placing his hands on my hips, he lifted them in the air. "Wrap your legs around my waist," he commanded as he kissed the inside of my thigh. He gently inched his way inside me with slow movements. Just the feeling of fullness, knowing that it was Sly inside me, sent my heart spinning. A rush of emotion hit like an unwanted guest and the tears began to pour.

"It's okay, baby, just let it go," Sly whispered.

"SLY!" I screamed as an explosion of emotion came to a head and surged to my core.

Sly must have felt my torture, because soon his arms were wrapped around me tightly and his movements increased faster and harder as he pushed deeper inside me. I opened my eyes to see the intensity in his face as he tried to hold back his own torment. We were like two lost souls coming together, feeding off of each other, getting stronger, knowing that we were meant to be together. Feeling his body tense, his groan of ecstasy mixed with the need to let go filled the space between us as his seed spilled inside me.

"How do you want that, baby?" I heard from the kitchen as I tried to concentrate on putting on the little make-up Peter provided for me.

"Over-easy will be fine," I yelled back.

I couldn't believe how much had changed within a twenty-four hour period. Sly was making breakfast for me, while I was finishing the final touches of placing mascara on my lashes. The earth-shattering connection we had last night brought a new light to what looked like a stormy day. Peter had contacted Sly on the burner phone, letting him know that the fight was called off. A rumor was spread that there was a chance a sting operation was in place and there was no information on who was the inside person planted by the feds. Even though it was only a rumor, I was pretty sure Peter started it. It must have been convincing enough to call the fight off.

Taking a last look at my handiwork, I accepted the way I looked, and went to where Sly was cooking up something delicious, by the way the smell filled the tiny house. Turning the corner, the view I was hit with just about took my breath away. Wearing nothing but a pair of faded jeans that hung low on his hips and a white apron that hung around his neck and tied in the back, he could have been a calendar model for one of those cooking shows my mom used to watch on television. He was that gorgeous.

"Mmm...," I hummed as I moved beside him to see what he had going on in the pan.

Turning his head, he gave me a tender kiss on my

temple and said, "Almost done, baby. I hope you're hungry."

"Am I ever," I answered with a smile.

I was totally in love with this man as I took my first bite of the meal he had prepared for us. Even though it was a simple breakfast consisting of eggs, bacon, and toast, it was amazing. I normally wasn't one to eat breakfast, but for some reason my stomach was protesting that it needed food.

Sly was staring at me like he had never seen anyone eat before, Looking up at him with a full mouth, I mumbled shamelessly, "What? I've worked up an appetite."

Shaking his head at me, he looked down at his own plate with a smile and resumed eating his eggs. I knew he was wondering if I was even chewing as quickly as I was shoving the food inside my mouth. I wasn't sure why I was so hungry. It had to have been the night of wonderful sex coupled with the strain of all the events that took place over the past week. All I knew was, I was hungry and I was ready to consume every last crumb of this amazing meal.

Drinking the last of my coffee, which was also amazing. I gathered the breakfast dishes and loaded them into the dishwasher. Sly came up behind be and gave me a tender kiss on the neck. "God, you smell good, baby," he said as he planted his nose in my hair.

"You can thank Peter for that, or maybe I should say Lilly," I replied.

Even though it wasn't the shampoo that I normally used, I had to admit that I liked the smell of it as well. Sly gave me one more chaste kiss, this time on the cheek, and headed to the living area. The last thing I heard was him greeting Peter on his cell. It made me curious as to why he would be calling him again, especially since he just talked to him. Drying my hands, I put my ear to the side of the wall to see if I could hear what they were taking about.

"Are you sure? I know... I should have told you. I was just protecting her," Sly stated.

I had no idea who he could have been talking about. All I knew was that whatever he was talking to Peter about involved me. I wasn't sure if I should confront him about what I heard or wait until he brought it up. Pushing my thoughts aside, I continued to hone in on the conversation.

"That's okay, Peter, I can handle it. I think it would be better coming from me instead of Nikki hearing it from someone else. I'm not sure how she is going to react."

I backed away from the wall, knowing that Sly had finished his call with Peter. The last thing I needed was to be caught eavesdropping on his private conversation. Although, if it was so private, I think he would have stepped outside or in a room that had a door. If he didn't tell me what he was hiding soon, I would be confronting him with what I heard.

CHAPTER SEVENTEEN

Sly

There was something that had changed in Nikki over the past couple of days. She was quiet and distant. Walking out of the house to the front pouch, I found her sitting on the step drinking a beer. I could tell that her thoughts were a million miles away. Taking a seat beside her, I took the bottle of beer from her and took a long draw. It didn't even faze her that I did.

"Hello, earth to Nikki," I finally said.

Standing, she tried to go back inside the house, but there was no way I was going to let her leave. Grabbing her arm, I pulled her against me to force her to stop. As much as she was fighting me, she finally knew she couldn't win. It was only after she smacked me with her fist across my cheek that I had to let go.

Nikki ran to the front door before I even knew what hit me. *"Damn, that girl has a mean punch,"* I thought to myself as I pushed from the step to follow her. By the time I got inside, she was already in the bathroom with the door locked. Unfortunately for her, that wasn't going to stop me from getting inside. I knew how the locks worked on these old doors. Reaching above my head, I felt for the master key to open the door. I hit pay dirt when the key fell to the floor in front of me.

Working the lock as quietly as I could, I finally got it open and was greeted by a surprised look on her face. Nikki was sitting on the toilet with her knees pulled to her chest. I never could understand the flexibility of women that allowed their body to be contorted that way.

Stepping in front of her, I placed my hands on her knees and looked at her sympathetically. "Nikki, you've been so closed off the past two days. I can't stand it any more. What's going on with you?"

"I think you need to be asking yourself that question, Sly. What are you keeping from me?" she questioned with a look of despair.

The only reason she would be asking that is if she heard my conversation with Peter. Standing to my feet, I held out my hand. "I'll tell you, but can we please not talk about it in the bathroom while you're sitting on the commode?"

I could have sworn I saw a slight smile when she looked up at me. Taking her by the hand, I led her out of the bathroom and to the living room. Sitting on the couch, I faced her, giving her the explanation she should have had two days ago.

"This isn't easy for me, Nikki. I think you already know how much I care about you." Taking a deep breath, I ran my hand through my hair, more nervous than I had ever been. "I had Peter look into your past for me. You have to understand, I didn't know what was going on with you. You were being so secretive. It was killing me not knowing about the girl I was falling hard for."

"Sly, you shouldn't have gone behind my back. Why would you do that?" she asked with conviction.

"I didn't know you were going to tell me about your past. Most everything that Peter found out, I already knew from you," I admitted. "But there are some things that you didn't know, like the way your mom died and the reason your father did."

"What are you talking about, Sly?" she stared at me with a confused look.

I didn't even know where to begin, so I figured from the beginning was the best option. "Remember when you told me that Carlos appeared at your door one day, just out of the blue, claiming to be your uncle?"

"Yeah," she replied.

"There was a reason he was there. The debt your

father owed Carlos was forgiven in exchange for one thing. The one thing he couldn't get himself."

"I don't understand?" Nikki confessed.

"It was your mom," I said, waiting for Nikki's reaction.

Placing my hand on her chin, I made sure she looked at me. "Nikki, please look at me."

When her eyes fell upon mine, I continued. "The minute Carlos set eyes on your mom, he fell in love with her. He wanted her and he would do anything to have her. He told your father the only way he could pay for his stupidity was to give up your mom to him."

"Who does that, Sly?" she asked, not believing what she was hearing.

"Carlos Giordano. He was so powerful that anything he wanted, he got." I stopped, making sure she was still with me. "Anyway, your dad wouldn't have it, so Carlos took it into his own hands and took her. She ended up pregnant. My guess is that he raped her. He was so obsessed with her, and when he found out that she was pregnant, it was icing on the cake. He thought for sure she would give him a son, only it never happened. She lost the baby. He was never going to give up. He tried to have another child with her. He never knew that she could never give him the son he wanted. Having you was the only child she would ever bear. She couldn't stand giving him a child, so she made sure she would never get pregnant again."

"I can't listen to this anymore. Not only did he take something sacred from my mom, he also took it from me. I hate him so much. I wish he was dead." Nikki was filled with so much anger that she pushed away from me and ran out the front door.

"Nikki, wait, please." I yelled.

"Leave me alone, Sly, I need to think," she choked as she took off down the dirt road.

~****~

I waited for what seemed like forever for Nikki to come back. It was getting dark and I was beginning to get worried. This had been the second time she had got away from me. I guess being an MMA fighter taught you to be quick on your feet. Grabbing my jacket, knowing she would be cold, I left the house to see if I could find where she might have gone. I knew she went down the dirt road leading to the main road, so that was my first move. I thought about taking the Camaro, but going on foot would be the best option, especially if she veered off the road into the wooded area.

Heading down the road, I looked through the trees to see if I could see her. I called out to her several times with no response. I was really getting worried now. I could barely see where I was going and I neglected to grab a flashlight when I left the house. Thinking that it was best to head back to the house, I heard her small voice. "Hey." she said.

"Jesus Christ, Nikki. Do you realize how worried

I was for you?" I questioned her.

"I know, I just needed to wrap my brain around what you said," she responded.

Walking over to her, I wrapped my coat around her shoulders and began walking with her back to the house. Pulling her closer to my side and giving her a light kiss on the head, I said softly, "Don't ever do that again."

There were no words from her so I was pretty sure she got the message. We walked in silence, hearing only the sound of the crunching gravel under our feet. There was still a lot that I needed to tell her about what Peter had found out. I knew she wouldn't be able to take any more bad news so I decided to feed her and get her beneath me and hold her tight while making sweet passionate love to her.

When we finally got back to the house, it seemed that Nikki was much calmer. Opening the door for her, I asked, "Are you hungry?" knowing that she was probably starving after being gone for so long.

"A little, but for now I just want to take a shower," she answered, looking over at me like she had more to say.

"What is it, Nikki?" I asked, concerned.

"When I'm done with my shower, I want you to tell me everything you know about my mom and dad."

I nodded, thinking that what I had to finish telling her might be too much for her. As soon as she was out of sight, I headed to the kitchen and pulled open the fridge. Popping the top off of a beer bottle, I took a long swig and leaned my body against the counter, trying to come up with an easy way to tell her that Carlos killed her parents. Even though he covered his tracks pretty good, there was still someone he forgot about. Namely, my father.

Drinking the last of my beer, I tried to digest how my father got caught up with Carlos. It could have been that he was in the right place at the right time to witness both deaths. He was there for a reason. I just wasn't sure why.

Pushing from the counter, I walked back to the bedroom to find Nikki drying her hair with a towel. The only thing she had on was a pair of lacy panties and one of my t-shirts that hung to the middle of her toned thighs. The minute she bent over, my dick got so hard, I thought it was going to burst right out of my jeans. She had the nicest ass I had ever seen. There was no way I could resist her anymore. Moving behind her, I placed my hands on her hips. Her body flew upward in surprise, causing her tight little ass to rub against my hard cock. Turning her head, she caught the look on my face and wrapped her arms around my neck. My head fell to her shoulder, taking in the scent of her freshly washed hair. God, how I loved the smell of her. Focusing in on her chest, the thin material of my t-shirt displayed the perfection of her nipples as they brushed against the material.

Lowering my hands from her hips, I took hold of her shirt and lifted up over her damp hair. The way her hair flowed down her back made me want to take her even more. I thought about running my hands through the soft curls and gripping it between my fingers while I pressed my cock deep inside her.

When her head fell back against my chest, I could only kiss the soft flesh of her neck before spinning her around and lifting her completely off the floor. With a hunger I didn't know existed, I pressed her body against the wall and within seconds my mouth was devouring every inch of her velvety skin.

I could hear her small whimpers of pleasure as her hands glided through my hair, pulling me closer to her body. Releasing one of my hands from holding her, I reached for my zipper and worked my pants down my legs. There was no way I was about to let go of her, so the cute skimpy panties she had on tore in two as I ripped them from her body.

My finger could feel her wetness as I slipped it inside her slick pussy. The hold she had on my finger told me that she was close. Lapping up her juices, I removed my finger from inside her and brought it to her lips. Her lips parted, sucking and licking every drop.. It was the sexiest thing I had ever seen, watching her sweet mouth move in such an enticing way.

Lowering her to the floor, I took hold of her waist and gently turned her around so that she was now facing the wall. With her ass bare and ready for me, I couldn't help but plant my open hand on the smooth white flesh that was destined to be a pretty shade of pink. I heard a small groan, but knew it was from pleasure and not pain. By the time I had finished spanking her, the color of her ass was a dark shade of pink. It was beautiful. The last woman I spanked didn't take it as well. Matter of fact, she ended up slapping me across the face.

Smiling to myself, I slowly entered Nikki, watching her honey coat my cock. The way her ass looked and the way my cock glistened was such a turn-on. Pushing to her center, I could feel her walls begin to tense. The tight grip she had on me was going to take me before I was ready. Licking my finger, I followed the curve of her ass and slid my finger between her cheeks until I found her tight pucker. With the tip of my finger, I began working it inside the tight hole. Feeling her body tense, I leaned over and whispered, "Relax, baby, I got this."

Feeling her relax, I continued slowly pushing my finger inside. "God, you're so tight, baby," I announced, with a sigh of satisfaction.

"Sly," I heard her whisper.

With my cock buried deep inside her and my finger planted in her tight ass, it made her even tighter as I inched my way deeper. Grasping her hip with my free hand, I used her hips as I dominated her movements, while guiding her body back as I propelled further inside. Her hips began moving more freely, accepting me. Seated fully within her walls, a moan of pleasure filled the space as her release took over. With the warmth of her juices coating my cock, the need to let go hit me like a tornado. My body shook with force, sending me in an upward spiral, leaving only the feeling of pure ecstasy in its wake.

Working up an appetite, we finished off two frozen pizzas. Once our bellies were full, at least Nikki's was since she ate most of it herself, we headed back to the bedroom for round two. I was right behind her as the soft sound of knocking came from the front door. Leaving to check the door, I turned to her and asked, "I wonder who that could be?"

Nikki shrugged her shoulders and headed to the bedroom. Waiting until she was gone, I reached into the drawer of the end table where I had placed the gun that Peter gave me. I had no way of knowing who was on the other side other than to ask, "Who's there?"

When there was no answer, I checked the deadbolt to make sure it was locked. Backing away from the door. I headed to the kitchen to the door that led to the back of the house. Carefully opening it so Nikki wouldn't hear, I stepped outside and headed around the side of the house to see if I could tell who was at the front door. Peeking around the corner of the porch, my eyes stilled with surprise. Never in a million years did I expect to see what I did.

A.L. Long

CHAPTER EIGHTEEN

Nikki

"Sly, you can't leave him out there. He'll die," I pleaded.

"Baby, you don't know where he has been and what he might be carrying. He could be infested with disease or something," Sly argued.

"I don't care, I'm bringing him in." There was no way I was going to leave a defenseless animal out in the dark, cold and maybe hurt.

Grabbing a blanket from the bedroom closet, I headed to the front door. It didn't surprise me that Sly was right behind me. When I opened the door, the poor little guy was looking up at me with the saddest eyes any dog could lay upon you. Lifting him from the porch, I held on to him as I wrapped his body in the blanket. Setting him on the chair, I went to the kitchen to get him some water.

Placing the bowl on the floor, I took him from the chair and placed him in front of the water. It didn't take him long before he was drinking the water, "Take it easy, little guy. You're going to make yourself sick," I said softly as I pet his matted fur.

I think Sly must have thought I was nuts, talking to a dog who had no idea what I was saying. It didn't matter that the little dog couldn't understand me, he knew I was there to help him by the tone of my voice, and that was all that mattered.

As I was taking care of the little dog, which I had no idea of even the breed, Sly was in the kitchen. It was when I smelled the scent of eggs that I realized he was making something for the dog to eat. I knew he wasn't as heartless as he pretended to be. He cared for the little dog as much as I did. Bringing a plate with a good portion of scrambled eggs on it, Sly placed it on the floor beside his bowl of water. At first the dog just looked up at Sly with sad eyes and then over to me. Taking a little of the egg in my hand, I held it out for him and waited for him to take it from me. When he finally did, he ate it all and continued licking my hand.

As we sat watching the little dog consume the food, my heart broke not knowing how long he had been alone out there. Lost with nowhere to go. My thoughts were broken when Sly picked up the empty plate and headed to the kitchen. I knew it had to be getting late. I pet the little guy one more time before I stood and folded the blanket so that he would have a comfortable place to sleep.

As we got ready for bed, I peeked out the door to make sure the little dog was okay. I could see that he was laying on the blanket. For a moment I thought he might have passed away, but he adjusted his position and fell back to sleep. Knowing that he was okay, I walked over to the bed where Sly was already pulling back the comforter. Sliding in beside him, he pulled me closer to his side and said softly, "That dog is going to need a name if you are planning on keeping it. He is also going to need some real food and care."

I didn't say a word, I only rolled over and kissed Sly, basically thanking him for understanding how I felt. Tomorrow the little dog would have a name and get checked out. But most of all, he would be loved.

~****~

I tried tugging the covers up over my shoulders, but was unable to move them. It was like they might have been caught under something. Lifting my head, I found out what was preventing me from getting the covers. It was white and brown, very furry, and weighed about twenty pounds, with the cutest puppy eyes I had ever seen. The dog must have sensed that I was awake, because he began slowly inching his body up the bed until his head was resting on my pillow. There was a slight groan from Sly that I had never heard before. I suspected it was because the dog was now separating us and taking up most of the room on the bed.

I wasn't sure how the poor thing got up on the bed in the first place, being in the frail condition he was in last night, but he seemed like a normal, healthy dog. I could tell that Sly wasn't very happy sharing the bed with a dog.

Looking over at Sly, I thought of a name that would fit this perfect little guy. "Romeo," I said with excitement."

"What?" Sly asked.

"Romeo. That's what his name is. It fits him perfectly, don't you think?"

"I think 'Pain in the ass' is a more suitable name for the little mutt," Sly admitted.

"Don't say that, he can understand you,"

"Right," Sly replied, moving to the edge of the bed. "I need some coffee."

I knew Sly wasn't happy about the fact that Romeo was making himself at home on our bed. I was pretty sure it was a one-time thing. Scooting off of the bed, I looked behind me to find that Romeo had jumped off as well. His little body rubbed up against my leg like he was telling me something. Putting on a pair of pants, I headed to the front of the house to take Romeo outside to do his thing. It was amazing how much better he looked from last night. I was beginning to think that he might have just been hungry and weak from no food or water in his body.

As I waited for for Romeo to do his thing, I heard the front door open. Looking over my shoulder, I saw Sly standing there holding two cups of coffee. Handing one to me, he stood beside me as I took a sip of the hot liquid. It tasted better than any coffee at the Happy Cow. It was then that it dawned on me that I did it again. I took off without letting Erin know where I was going. There was no way I was ever going to keep my job. I was unreliable.

Watching Romeo sniff around the dirt, Sly said, "We should probably think about getting him some food and to a vet."

I was pretty much in agreement with him. Calling Romeo, we went back into the house. Sly and I decided it would be quicker to take a shower together, only it didn't happen that way. With his hands all over my body and mine all over his, it was no surprise that we ended up having a quickie. It was only after Sly turned off the water and pulled back the shower curtain that he saw Romeo sitting on the tile floor looking right at him. If I didn't know better, I would have thought that Romeo was jealous of Sly. I pushed away the thought and hurried out of the shower, dried myself off, and hurried into the bedroom to put some clothes on.

~****~

I was so glad to leave the vet's office. All of the cats and dogs that were waiting to be seen looked so sad. It was if they all knew that this was a bad place. It was good to hear that Romeo was fine. The only thing wrong with him was that he was a little dehydrated. Spending an hour at the vet's and then another hour at the grocery store, I was ready to get back to the house. I think Romeo was too. I think he hated the fact of being left in the car. Even though I sat with him, he was getting very antsy.

On our drive back to the house, I could have sworn I saw something in the corner of my eye that looked like a black Escalade. Scanning the street that we were on, I let the thought leave my mind and chalked it up to paranoia. We had been away for five days and hadn't seen or heard from anyone except Peter. I was beginning to think that the whole fight thing was forgotten and we could go back to New York.

Focusing my attention on the road, I held Romeo in my lap. I think it was more for security than anything else. I don't know what came over me, but there was some unfinished business with Sly, and right now was a good time as any to find out what else he knew about my mom and dad.

"So what else did you need to tell me?" I asked, petting Romeo on his back.

"I don't think now is a really good time to get into it, Nikki. When we get home, I'll tell you everything."

Leaning back in my seat, I was about to argue with Sly, but knew that he was right. Discussing my mom and dad while he was driving was probably not a very good idea. I waited this long to hear what he had to say, a few more minutes wasn't going to make a difference.

When we finally pulled up to the house, Romeo was going crazy. He was barking like something was going on. He jumped over the console and into the back seat. His sights were set on something out the back window. Sly and I both looked in the side mirrors to see if we could tell what he was barking at. There was nothing there. Turning my head, I looked out the back window, but I was still unable to see what got Romeo's attention.

Sly opened his door and pulled his seat forward so

that Romeo could be let out. He darted out of the car and in the direction of where he was barking. It was weird the way he was acting. It was like there was some sort of force field in place, because when he got five feet from the car, just like that, he stopped in his tracks. It was the strangest thing I had ever witnessed.

Getting out of the car, I walked over to Romeo and knelt down beside him. "What is it Romeo? What do you see?" I asked, knowing he wouldn't be able to answer.

Romeo's barking turned into cries and he slowly turned and headed to the house. Something spooked him, but as Sly and I looked around, there was nothing there. Unloading the trunk, we headed inside the house. Sly began putting groceries away while I got Romeo's food dish ready. From the time we got to the house to the time Romeo went inside the house, he was acting very jumpy. This was odd behavior, even for a dog. As I finished filling Romeo's dish, a call came in on Sly's phone. I could tell by Sly's movements that whoever he was talking to was making him uneasy. Looking at me, he gave me a worried look before heading to the front door and leaving the house.

~****~

The silence was killing me as we pulled down the covers on the bed. The conversation that Sly had earlier made his mood change. Unable to stand it any longer, I asked point blank, "Are you going to tell me who called earlier or are you going to continue being pissed off?"

"We need to talk, Nikki," he demanded.

"Ooookay," I said, uncertain what he was getting at as I looked into his brown eyes. "What is this about, Sly?"

Taking a seat on the bed, he rounded the other side and took his place beside me. Taking my hand, his eyes fell to his lap. It was like he couldn't bring himself to look at me. Rubbing my hand, he was beginning to worry me. When his eyes finally met mine, I was afraid to hear what he had to say, so when he said, "Mandy," my heart fell to my stomach.

I never told Sly about her, so it made me wonder how he found out about her. This was one memory I tried so hard to forget, but to hear Sly say her name brought everything back. "How do you know that name?"

"Why didn't you tell me about her, Nikki?" he asked, letting go of my hand and rising to his feet.

"I never told you because it's part of my life I wanted to lock away and never look at again," I confessed.

"You should have told me," he paused, taking his place on the bed again. "Did anyone else know about what happened to her besides Carlos?"

"I don't think so. Carlos said he would take care of it. When they pulled her from the ring they advised all of the spectators that she was okay, I knew she wasn't. I knew exactly what I did to her the minute my fist landed on the side of her head."

"Well, someone else found out about it. There's a warrant out for your arrest," Sly confessed.

"Sly, that happened over ten years ago, why would they have a warrant out for me now, after all this time?" I asked in a panic.

"There is no time limit on murder, Nikki, at least that is what they are accusing you of."

"Murder? Are you shitting me? It was an accident." I couldn't believe what I was hearing. "*How could they charge me with murder after all this time? It just didn't make sense.*"

"Remember when I told you there was something you needed to know about your mom and dad?"

"Yeah, I remember." I replied, still unable to wrap my head around what Sly just told me.

"Carlos was behind their deaths. Somehow, he

found out what your mom did so she would never be able to have another child. Not only did he blame her, he also blamed your father. He felt like your father went back on his promise to repay him. Carlos ordered the hit on your mom and then your dad. Taking the one thing she loved from your mom was his ultimate revenge. He made her watch while one of his men shot your father in the head. Then Carlos took the same gun and shot your mom himself."

"How do you know all this, Sly? How?" I pleaded as the tears came pouring down.

"I know because..." he paused like he was afraid to say what needed to be said.

"How?" I demanded.

"I know, because my father was there."

I didn't understand what Sly was saying. Why would his father be there? It didn't make any sense. Trying to sort out the information, it finally hit me. "The only way your dad could have known is if he worked for Carlos. Oh, my God, is that it? Did your father work for Carlos Giordano?"

CHAPTER NINETEEN

Sly

I didn't know how to tell Nikki the truth. The truth was my father didn't work for Carlos, but he did work for Angelo Conti, who was not only a rival, but also Carlos' cousin.

"Sly, please answer me. Did your father work for Carlos?" she asked again.

"No, he didn't."

"Then how was he there? Who did he work for?"

Standing again, I ran my hand through my hair,

pacing the short distance between the bed and the bathroom. Turning to face Nikki, I stopped and took in a deep breath. "My father was there because he worked for Angelo Conti." Looking over to Nikki, I began explaining, seeing the confusion on her face. "Angelo Conti is the cousin of Carlos. Something happened between the two families and it ended up in a rivalry between them. My father was instructed to keep close tabs on Carlos and find out what his next move was going to be, only he got more than he bargained for. As much as I hate my father for the life he chose, there is no way he could have known about the plan to kill your parents."

"What did he see, Sly?" she asked.

"Everything. He saw both of your parents facing each other on their knees with gags over their mouths and their hands tied behind their backs. One of Carlos' men shot your father while your mom watched. He could tell by the look on her face that she just died herself. My father couldn't hear what Carlos said to her, but whatever it was, it was the last thing he said before he kissed her on the forehead and then shot her himself. My dad said he had seen enough. He got the hell out of there and waited until they cleaned up the mess and went back to their car. My father assumed that Carlos had their bodies dumped in the water close to the dock where they were killed."

"What does this have to do with Mandy?" she asked.

"My father, as much as I hate him, and I'm not agreeing with what he did, is the person that saw what happened that night in the ring. He had no idea that you were the same same girl that I fell in love with."

"Wait. Are you saying that your father contacted the police about knowing what happened that night in the ring? This is so messed up, Sly. Why would he do that?"

"Revenge," I stated.

"Revenge, are you kidding me? I can't believe this shit," she yelled as she threw her hands in the air and left the room.

I knew that the information I had wasn't going to sit well with her, especially knowing that I may have prevented this whole thing. I needed to make her understand that I had no control over what my father was going to do. Running after her, I had to let her know.

Nikki didn't go very far. She was in the kitchen pouring herself a glass of wine, which she pulled from one of the cupboards. I was with her on this one, only I needed something a lot stronger than wine. Going to the same cupboard, I reached towards the back and pulled out a bottle of whiskey that I found earlier when I was putting away the groceries. As I filled my glass about three-quarters full, I gazed over to Nikki as she downed her wine and was ready to pour another glass.

Placing my hand on the bottle, I focused on her hand as it began shaking as she poured the wine. "Let me do that," I offered.

"Everything is so messed up, Sly,"

I pulled her into me, knowing that this was all

messed up, but that it wasn't the end of the world. There had to be a way to fix this before her world came crashing down. "Everything will be okay, baby. We will figure this out," I said, lifting her chin and placing my lips over hers. Her hand wrapped around mine, needing to hold onto something that was real.

Breaking the kiss, she looked up at me with tear-drenched eyes and asked, "Did you mean what you said? Do you really love me?"

Lifting her from the floor, I answered with a definite, "Hell, yeah."

My lips fell upon hers once again, only now she knew exactly how I felt. There was no way in hell I was ever going to let anything happen to her. Leaving our drinks, I carried her to the bedroom, where I planned to worship her all night, only this time there were not going to be any interruptions. Closing the door, I took her over to the bed and placed her gently down, Propping my body on my elbows, I stared at her, seeing for the first time the woman I loved more than anything look back at me with desperation.

Dipping my head, I kissed her tenderly on her swollen lips, tasting a hint of salt from the tears she shed. Tearing away from her long enough to remove her top, I continue to feast on her as I slowly moved down her body. Holding her breast with my hand, I gently caressed the soft flesh until her nipple peaked through the thin material of her bra. Lowering the cup of her bra, my mouth found her nipple and began licking and sucking the taut bud. Her back began to arch, letting me know that my assault on her breast was giving her the pleasure she needed. This is the way it would always be. To be the only man she would ever want. Moving further down her body, I soaked up every inch of her velvety skin as I trailed one kiss after another down her body.

Losing all control to be gentle, I lifted her hips from the bed and pulled the black leggings from her body, along with the tiny thong she was wearing underneath. Removing my own clothes, I positioned my body between her toned legs and placed them on either side of my shoulders. Lost in her scent, I lowered my head and began consuming her sweet honey that was waiting for me to devour it. Her folds were so slick with her juices that my tongue moved with ease between them, lapping up every drop of her essence. Moving my tongue to her swollen nub, I slid my finger between her folds to find that they effortlessly slid inside her tight channel.

My cock pulsated to point of almost being painful. All I wanted at that moment was to taste her, feel her, worship her. It didn't matter that my own desire was about to take control. I wanted to give her everything that her body needed. Working my finger in and out of her, I began to feel the movement of her hips as she pressed against me. "That's it, baby. Feel everything that I am going to give you."

I heard a small moan as she increased her movements. Taming her need to come, I pulled my finger from inside her and moved up her body. Taking her nipple in my mouth, I circled the hard peak while caressing the other one between my fingers; pinching and tugging on the sensitive bud. Her moans became louder. I was filled with so much desire for this woman that I was about to lose my own self-control. Giving her a passionate kiss on the lips, I positioned my shaft between her legs where I knew her entrance would be ready to consume me. Claiming her as mine, I marked her with my mouth, sucking and kissing her breast as I gently pushed inside her. The minuted I entered her, her walls tightened around my cock, sending a surge of pleasure down my cock to the base of my sac. Moving slowly, I wanted to savor this feeling. The harder she pushed against me, the slower my movements were.

"Sly, please," rang from her mouth as her need to come escalated.

"Not yet, baby," I whispered, kissing the area right below her earlobe, which I knew would send her over the edge.

Moving my hands under her hips, her walls tightened like a vice grip on my cock, sending me closer to my own release as she exploded, unwilling to hold on any longer. My movements increased, feeling the warmth of her essence surround me. Pumping harder and deeper, my cock began to pulsate, synchronizing with the beating of my heart.

Like a sign from above, her scream of ecstasy filled the room and my walls came down, spilling my seed deep inside her. When our bodies finally relaxed and our breathing evened out, I swiped away her damp hair and confessed, "I love you, baby."

Her arms wrapped around me and she planted her head on my shoulder, just holding me as tightly as she could. Even though she didn't say that she loved me back, I knew without a doubt the feeling she had for me. Kissing her on the forehead, I got off of her and slipped into the bathroom to grab a washcloth. When I returned, she was already asleep. Careful not to wake her, I took the warm cloth and slid it gently between her legs. She must have felt the warmth because her legs opened for me and a soft request came from her lips. "More."

I knew exactly what she wanted, only this time it would not be rushed, I would be a man making love to the woman he loved. Slow, easy, passionate.

~****~

The sun was barely peeking through the window when I heard an annoying sound coming from the door. It almost sounded like someone was trying to claw their way into the room. It was then that I remembered the new addition to our home. Sitting up, I leaned over and gave Nikki a sweet peck on the cheek before getting up to see what damage Romeo did to the door. Even though he was a small dog, the way he was going at it, I knew there was going to be bare wood showing on the door frame.

As soon as I opened the door, he darted to the bed, hiding his body under the covers. I was surprised to find that he had done minimal damage to the door, Walking out of the bedroom into the living room was another story. Every throw pillow that was on the couch was shredded to pieces. I couldn't believe that a dog his size could be so destructive.

Before Nikki got out of bed, not only did I have a little talk with Romeo, I also managed to clean up the mess he made with the pillows. Hearing her footsteps as I put the last of the pillow stuffing into a garbage bag, I stowed it away in the pantry until I could get rid of it.

With her eyes barely open and her hair in a messy something or other on top of her head, she was still beautiful. Even if she wore a gunny sack, she would still have been the most gorgeous woman I had ever seen. "What's going on with Romeo? He came in the bedroom with his tail between his legs," she asked, yawning as she spoke.

Opening the pantry door, I showed her exactly why the stupid mutt was feeling so guilty. Looking down at him with an angered look, she pointed her finger at him and shook it. "You are a bad dog, Romeo."

Just like when he came to the room, he sauntered off with his tail between his legs and headed to the bedroom.

"I already told him that, baby. You have to remember, he's still considered a puppy according to the vet," I reminded her.

Walking up to me, she bumped my hip with hers, letting me know that she wanted me to move over. Taking a mug from the cupboard, she poured herself a cup of coffee and headed to the couch, which was now bare because it no longer had the pillows on it. Joining her on the couch, there was a knock at the door. I could only wonder who would be knocking at the door this early in the morning, for one. And for another, who even knew we were here except for Peter and the guys?

Opening the door, I was speechless. It made sense. The only thing I could think to say was, "Come in."

When the deputy sheriff peered over to where Nikki was sitting, he asked in a deep voice, "Nikki Jennings?"

Nikki stood and acknowledged him. "Yes, can I help you?"

"You will need to come with me. You are being charged with the murder of Mandy Morgan."

CHAPTER TWENTY

Nikki

This had to have been the scariest thing I had ever been through. After being read my Miranda rights, I was taken back to Central Booking in Brooklyn, where I was booked, fingerprinted, and escorted to a six-by-eight cell. I was told that I was entitled to one phone call, but I didn't know who I was going to call. Sly was working on getting my bail money. My bail hearing was set for tomorrow at noon, and I wasn't even sure if they would let me out.

Sitting on the hard bed, all I could think about was how my life had changed within a matter of hours. One minute I was snuggled close to Sly in a warm comfortable bed, and the next, I was sitting on a hard mattress with a blanket that couldn't have been any thicker than a piece of tissue paper. All I wanted was to be out of here. I tried to think of anything else but being in here, but when a police officer came to my cell letting me know that I had a visitor, I was back to reality. I had no idea who it could be, considering that I wasn't allowed any visitors until tomorrow.

Being placed in a small room, I waited for whoever was coming to see me. Hearing the door open, I waited until whoever it was, was in full view before I greeted them. The minute I saw him, I should have gotten up from my chair and requested to be taken back to my cell.

"What are you doing here, Carlos?" I said between gritted teeth.

"Is that any way to talk to the one person who happens to be your ticket out of here?" he pointed out sarcastically.

"I don't want your help. I know who you are and I know what you did."

"I think it best for you to think twice about that, Nikki. I think maybe you have forgotten the reason you're in here in the first place. What you should be asking yourself is, do I want to get out of here?"

I couldn't help but wonder why Carlos was so special and how he thought he would be able to get me out of here without a hearing. "What do you want?" I asked.

"It is not a matter of what I want as much as it is what you want. I am pretty sure you don't want to be spending the rest of your life behind bars," he reminded me.

"Once I let them know what really happened to Mandy, they'll see that it was an accident."

"That may be, Nikki, but what they will not understand is how you tried to cover her death up knowing that you two were fighting illegally."

"You were the one who covered it up. I'm done lying about this and not telling the truth about what happened that night. Sure, the fight was illegal, but I was only a child and I was forced to fight her," I seethed as I watched Carlos take his phone from his pocket.

"Are you sure you want to do that, Nikki?" he asked, swiping the screen on his phone and then playing a video.

As I watched and listened to what was going on in the video, I knew it was all a lie. Somehow, Carlos fabricated the video to show me as the one who covered up Mandy's death. It also showed that I ordered Carlos' men to take her from the ring. It was me in the video, but I know, for a fact, I never said those things.

"You know that isn't what happened, Carlos."

"Well, it certainly looks to me like you were the one who was making the demands. Matter of fact, I don't see myself anywhere in the video. As I recall, I wasn't even there."

"You liar," I yelled with hatred for this man as I rose and was ready to smack him across the face. Even though he hadn't put me here, he was just as guilty and he was going to use it to his advantage.

"Now, now, Nikki. You need to control that temper of yours," he stated as I backed off and sat back down in my seat. "You can make this all go away. All you have to do is do what I say and all of this can go away."

~****~

As the car pulled away from the police station. I kept wondering how Carlos managed to get the charges against me dropped. I hated this man sitting beside me so much that if I thought I could get away with killing him, I would have. He had me right where he wanted me. With the video still in his grubby hands, I had no other choice but to go with him. I had no idea where he was going to take me. The worst part of this whole thing was, for all Sly knew, I was still in jail awaiting my bail hearing tomorrow afternoon. I couldn't even contact him to let him know what happened.

Pulling into the circular drive, Carlos' driver got out of the car and came to my side, where he opened the door and stepped to the side to allow me to exit. I had never been to Carlos' house, but looking at the enormous mansion, all I could think about was how much dirty money bought this monstrosity.

Nudging me along, Carlos placed his hand on my lower back, letting me know that he wanted me to move. As much as I would have preferred to stay where I was, once again he had all the control. Waiting at the door was an older lady dressed in a black and white maid's uniform with her hands crossed and hanging down in front of her. When we got closer, she moved to the side and said, "Good evening, Mr. Giordano."

"Good evening, Agnes. Is everything ready for Ms. Jennings?" Carlos asked in a formal tone.

"Yes, sir, just as you asked." the maid replied.

Heading into the house, there was a round table in the entrance with a crystal vase full of roses, lilies, and baby's breath. It was very regal. Kind of like something you would see on a fancy house infomercial on how to decorate your home. The floor looked to be marble by the way it shone perfectly, with not a speck of dirt on it. Looking to the ceiling, I saw the largest three-tiered chandelier I had ever seen. It was absolutely breathtaking. As I was looking around, another gentleman entered the foyer, wearing the same black and white attire.

"Bishop, would you please show Ms. Jennings to her room?" Carlos asked with authority.

"Very well, sir," he paused. "This way, Ms. Jennings." The tall skinny gentleman, who had to be at least sixty, motioned to me as he stepped to the side.

Following him up the staircase, I took in my surroundings. As much as I hated Carlos, I had to admit he had good taste in mansions. The man in front of me, which I assumed was the butler, walked down a hallway and then turned to his right and opened a door. He reached inside the doorway and turned on the lights. When I got inside the room, I couldn't believe what I saw. It was the biggest bedroom I had ever seen. It was decorated in deep purple and black. Amazed by the room, I barely heard the butler leave.

Checking it out, I opened the first door that I saw, which ended up being the closet. My bedroom in my new apartment could have fit inside the large room. Not only was the size unbelievable, it had been filled with clothing that I would never wear or even have the need to wear. Whereas I was more of a jeans and t-shirt kind of girl, the closet was filled with dresses, gowns, and pantsuits.

Having seen enough of the closet, I stumbled to the next door, which turned out to be the bathroom. Once again, it was huge. There was not only a large shower that could easily fit four people inside, there was also a mammoth-sized tub that someone could get swallowed up in. Everything about this house was over the top. It was way more than I could handle.

Pulling me from my thoughts, there was a light knock on the door. Leaving the bathroom, I walked over to the door to find that the maid who was in the entrance earlier was standing outside holding some towels in her arms.

Stepping aside to let her in, her soft voice said, "Mr. Giordano thought you might want to freshen up before dinner. I brought you some fresh towels."

I was just about to take them from her when she spoke again. "I will draw you a bath, Miss."

Letting her do what she felt was necessary, I waited for her to finish as I listened to the water running in the bathroom. Pacing was the only thing I could do while I tried to think of what I was going to do. The first thing I needed to do was try to find a way to get in touch with Sly. This was going to take some doing, since there was no phone in the room and I couldn't just ask for one.

The maid appeared again and was about to assist me in getting ready for my bath by helping me undress. Never in my life have I ever let another woman undress me, and there was no way I was going to start now even if she was the maid. "I'll get undressed myself," I said sharply.

"Very well, my name is Agnes, please let me know if you need anything else. There is an intercom here…" she pointed out as she walked over to the wall by the door. "Just press the button and I will be up straight away."

I waited until 'Agnes' left the room before I began stripping my clothes off. When I went into the bathroom, not only were the towels she brought in laying on the counter, there was also a robe, a pair of peach lace panties with a matching bra, and a set of silk pajamas. *"Yep, I really need to get out of here,"* I said to myself as I dipped my foot in the water to make sure it wasn't too hot.

Sitting in the comfort of the hot water and the

fluffy bubbles, my body finally began to relax. I don't know if it was the warmth of the water or the sweet scent of cherry blossoms that had my tension easing. Closing my eyes, I tried to picture how this whole thing with Carlos was going to play out. He still hadn't told me what he wanted from me, and more than that, I still didn't how he managed to get me out of the police station so quickly.

It was then that the memory of the video entered my mind, I had no idea how he did it, but I knew that if I didn't do as he asked, he was going to use the video against me. It would be his leverage to keep me with him forever. I was never going to be able to break away from him. Realizing what my fate was going to be, the tears began to swell in my eyes. If only Sly was here. He would know how to help me get out of this. Even though I was with him just this morning, I missed him so much.

The water was getting cold, which signaled that it was time to get out. I could have stayed in the water forever if it meant that I could avoid having dinner with Carlos. I really didn't even have an appetite. The only thing I wanted to do was make a plan on how I was going to get in touch with Sly.

Pulling on the lacy panties and then the matching bra, it didn't surprise me that they fit perfectly. The silk pajamas that Agnes left for me also fit like they were made for me. I slid on the robe and slipped on the matching heeled slippers with a silky bow at the toe, and headed down to the main area of the house. I wasn't sure where dinner was going to be served, but I was pretty sure I would be running into someone that could show me the way. Taking a deep breath, I opened the door to the bedroom and headed into what was going to be my destiny.

CHAPTER TWENTY-ONE

Sly

I was so happy that Peter was able to get in touch with some people he knew to get Nikki out of jail. I knew that the charges against her were nothing more than a way to get to her. Aside from my father's part in her arrest, I was certain that Carlos, no doubt, had his hand in this as well. I just couldn't figure out how Angelo found us.

Walking to the parking garage and seeing my Jeep good as new reminded me Peter really knew how to take care of his own. I needed to make sure the favor was returned.

Driving to the police station, all I could think about was how frightened Nikki must have been spending the night in jail. Sure, she could put on a tough act, but I knew her well enough to know that she was falling apart inside.

After talking to Peter, we both decided it would be better if we met at the station. I couldn't have agreed more with him, seeing as how all I wanted to do when I got Nikki home was to devour every inch of her body. Pulling up to the station, I could see that Peter was waiting outside below the steps leading into the 66th precinct. There were a few police officers standing outside as well. My guess was that they were getting ready to go out on patrol. Crossing the street, I walked over to where Peter was standing. I got evil stares from the police officers, who were probably wondering what my business was at the police station.

Walking up the steps, we entered the precinct, where we were met by an officer that was standing behind the main counter. Peter walked up the counter and waited patiently until the officer finally acknowledged that he was there.

"Can I help you with something?" the officer asked, looking first at Peter, and then at me.

"You're holding a Ms. Nikki Jennings. She is supposed to be arraigned at noon. Can you let us know where the arraignment is being held?" Peter asked.

"Let me see," the officer paused as he looked up her name on his computer. "Looks like the charges against Ms. Jennings have been dropped. She was released yesterday afternoon."

I looked over to Peter, thinking that he knew something about this, but seeing the look on his face, he was just as surprised as I was. As we walked from the station, we held in our thoughts until we got outside.

"What the fuck, Peter?" I asked, confused as hell.

"You got me, bro. I have no idea what just happened," he replied.

"There is only one person I can think of that would have a hand in this: Carlos Giordano."

"I couldn't agree with you more." Peter confessed. "We just need to figure out where he might have taken her."

I got in my Jeep while Peter got in his Camaro and headed back to the shop to do some more digging on Carlos Giordano. I knew of one person that could help us out. As much as I hated asking anything of him, I knew he would be the one person that would be able to help.

Driving back to the shop, I pulled the one number I thought I would never need to contact. "Gus, I need your help."

~****~

I pulled up to the shop shortly after Peter, knowing my father would be arriving shortly. It gave me just enough time to fill Peter in on our surprise guest. Opening the door, Mike, Lou, and Ash were sitting on the couch shooting the shit, while Ryan was leaning against the wall talking on his cell. Peter was already in his office getting started on finding out more information on Carlos Giordano. Pulling up a chair in front of his desk, I leaned forward and ran my hands through my hair, knowing what I was about to tell him was going to blow his mind.

"My father, Gus Capelli, is going to help us out with this situation with Carlos Giordano." There was no way I was going to beat around the bush.

"Why would you think he would be able to help us, Sly?" he questioned.

"Because he works for Angelo Conti."

"Are you fucking serious, bro? Angelo Conti?"

"Yeah."

As Peter and I were talking, Ash stepped into the office and announced that my father had arrived. Staring at the door, I watched Ash leave and within minutes my father appeared. I couldn't think of two words to say to him, but I knew that I needed him more than ever. Taking a seat beside me, I introduced him to Peter. "Peter, this is my father, Gus Capelli."

"Nice to meet you, Mr. Capelli," Peter greeted him, holding his hand out.

My father held out his hand and said, "Please call me Gus. All my friends do."

I was about to tell him that Peter was never going to be his friend, especially after I told him the full story about my dad, which I knew would be coming up as soon as he left. Looking over to my father, I asked him with reservation. "Do you know where Carlos Giordano would take Nikki?"

"What is this about, son?" Gus said, accusingly, like I had done something.

"You are acting like this is about me. This is about Nikki and the shit life she has because of that lowlife son-of-a-bitch."

"Does this have to do with her mom and dad being murdered?" he asked.

"This has to do with the fact that you basically threw her under the bus and now there's the possibility that Carlos might be holding this over her as some sort of payment for something that she had no control over," I retorted.

"I told you I didn't know Nikki was the same girl from all those years ago. I was just doing what I was told. If you want to blame someone, blame Angelo Conti, he was the one who wanted to get even with Carlos."

An hour later, the truth about what really happened ten years ago finally came out, down to the last detail. There was even proof as to what really happened, and it seemed that Carlos had the only evidence proving that Mandy's death was a complete accident. Even though I would never be able to forgive my father for the life he chose to live, at least he was willing to share the information he had on Carlos to put him behind bars for life and set Nikki free from his control, once and for all. The only problem was getting our hands on it.

By the time my father left, we had a pretty good idea where Carlos might have taken Nikki. My father knew Carlos' estate like the back of his hand, having been assigned to him so many years ago. Getting to Nikki was going to be like breaking into Fort Knox the way my father had explained the security that he had. I knew that I needed to get her out of there, and where there was a will, there was a way. I just needed to find it.

Peter and I decided that we needed to see for ourselves this fortress that my father described. Deciding to take Peter's Camaro, we drove to the address that my father gave us, which was located just outside the city where all the upscale estates were located. I knew this area well enough to know there was one reason why people live this far out of the city. It was the privacy, and the fact that the majority of them were affiliated with the Mob in some form or another.

Peter parked just outside the gate of the mansion and cut the engine. It was dark enough outside that we could check out the estate without being noticed. We just needed to stay clear of the cameras that were positioned just outside the gate. Exiting the car, we crossed the street to see if there was anything we could determine once we got closer. Peter suggested that we walk around to the side of the brick wall to get a better look at what we would be up against once we were able to get past the walls.

With the brick wall surrounding the mansion, it didn't offer an easy entrance to the other side. Improvising, I crossed my hands and signaled for Peter to allow me to hoist him up to the top edge of the wall. As he stepped on my hand, he steadied his body by placing his hands on the wall, while I lifted him higher. Needing more height, Peter gestured to me with a thumbs up letting me know that he needed to get higher.

I don't know what he thought I could do, but I did my best to reposition my hand so that I could push him higher, at least high enough that he could look over the wall. Waiting for what seemed like forever, Peter finally whispered, "Fuck, bro. This is going to take some planning."

I had no idea what he was looking at, but I was pretty sure it was bad. "What do you see?"

"It's not good, that's for sure," he confessed.

Lowering him back down, we headed back to the car. I needed to know what he saw. There was no way we were going to leave until he told me. I needed to know what the hell I was up against.

Closing the door and heading away from the estate, I couldn't wait one more second, "So how bad is it?" I asked.

"Bad, Sly. Really bad," Peter confessed.

The more Peter told me about what he saw, I was beginning to think that we weren't going to be able to get inside. He pointed out that not only was there a guard at each entrance that he could see, the grounds were covered in motion sensors. The only way he knew this was by the dogs that were being led around the grounds by more guards, who were setting them off. There was no way we would be able to get inside without setting them off, unless we were invisible.

The only thing I could think of was how fucked we were, but more importantly, how screwed Nikki would be if we couldn't get her out of there. Once again, I thought to myself, *"Where there's a will, there's a way."*

When we got back to the shop, we called all the guys together and began working on a plan to get inside the estate. My dad wasn't lying when he said that Carlos' estate was more secure than Fort Knox. There had to be a way that we could get inside. Nothing was inaccessible, at least where Jagged Edge Security is concerned, that is. We had tackled much harder places to gain access to.

Once everyone arrived, Peter began explaining to them what we were up against. I could see by the looks on their faces, they weren't too confident that this was going to be a successful mission. I knew they all had their doubts, but there was no way I was going to leave Nikki in the hands of Carlos Giordano.

"Guys, do you remember why we agreed to work for Jagged Edge? We have always stuck together and have never let each other down, no matter how difficult or dangerous the task. We are talking about the life of a person that needs to be saved. Carlos Giordano has got to be stopped. If we don't stop him, who knows who his next victim will be when he is done with Nikki. Do you get me?" I pleaded with them.

As they looked over to each other and then to me, Ash stood, and commanded, "Sly's right, you guys. We have never said no to a mission just because we felt it was impossible. We have always made the impossible, possible. This is who we are."

I watched as the guys listened to Ash. Most all of them shaking their heads in agreement. I knew that they would never let me down. Through and through, we were brothers, and brothers look out for each other no matter what the circumstances, but most of all, no matter what the danger.

CHAPTER TWENTY-TWO

Nikki

I was so glad that I got through dinner with no sight of Carlos. The last thing I wanted to do was have any kind of conversation with the man like we were family. Finishing my last bite, I heard some voices coming from the other room. One of them I recognized right away as Carlos'. Just the thought of him being here made my stomach turn. Feeling like I was about to lose everything I ate, I rushed to the door leading to the kitchen, hoping that I wouldn't end up spilling my guts on the marble floor.

There were only two servants in the massive kitchen. The only thing I cared about was finding the sink. It didn't even matter that the two women were staring at me like I had grown a set of horns. With little time left, I spotted the sink and went over to it as quickly as I could. Bending over the stainless steel basin, I let the gates open. With the amount of noise I was making, I was positive that it could be heard from the dining room just through the door.

When I spilled everything I could, I turned on the faucet and cupped my hands under the cool water. Splashing it on my face, I heard one of the women say to the other, "I didn't think that the duck was dry."

If they only knew that it wasn't the meal that had my stomach doing cartwheels, it was the fact that Carlos was home and I couldn't stand to be near him. Grabbing the towel that one of the woman handed me, I dried off my face and said, "Thank you."

Heading back to the dining area, I looked down at the empty plate, realizing that I forgot something. Turning back, I opened the door and said, softly, "The duck was perfect."

The only response was the smiles stretching across the two women's faces in relief. The voices I heard earlier were no longer in the entrance of the big house. Whoever Carlos was talking to must have left, or maybe he thought it would be better to take the conversation elsewhere. Either way, I knew it was my chance to get back to my room and lock myself inside, safe and away from Carlos.

Removing my slippers, I rushed up the stairs, taking the steps two at a time. All I wanted was to get to my room, brush my teeth, and lay in bed. Maybe if I went to sleep, my dreams would take me anywhere but here.

As I opened the door, my body just about fell to the floor as Carlos peered at me with his dark gaze. Sitting in a chair near the window, he stood and walked over to me. I wanted to back away from him, but the door was at my back, keeping me from moving.

Touching my cheek, he rubbed his thumb along my cheekbone and asked, "My dear Nykia, what am I going to do with you?"

"For starters, you can stop calling me that. I haven't gone by that name since the day you took me," I seethed, turning my head from his touch.

His mood changed and he turned from me and went to the chair he was previously sitting in, only this time he didn't sit, he just gazed out the window to the grounds, probably inspecting his security.

Pulling him from whatever he was thinking, I blurted out, "What do you want, Carlos?"

"That seems to be your only concern these days." he said, turning his body towards me. "You will need to be ready in the morning for your training. You only have a week to prepare."

"Training for what?"

"I don't know what game you're playing, Nykia, but I do know that your boyfriend and his friends at the security company he works for... Jagged Edge, I believe, had something to do with the fight not happening. It will not happen again. You will be ready and you will be fighting Black Jewel."

Stepping away from the door to let him leave, I waited until he was gone before I gave him the bird and called him a *'lowlife son-of-a-bitch'* under my breath. Walking over to the bathroom, I angrily put a dollop of toothpaste on my toothbrush and began frantically brushing my teeth with a vengeance. I was so angry at myself for allowing Carlos to get to me the way that he did. He was nothing to me.

Turning down the bed, I removed my robe and slipped under the covers, hiding myself from the rest of the world. Looking to the ceiling, I couldn't help but think about what Sly was going to do once he found out that I had been released and the charges against me were dropped. I knew that he was smart enough to know that something like that just doesn't happen, especially when there is a murder charge against you.

Closing my eyes and thinking of something else was a lot harder than I thought it would be. My mind kept drifting to all the things that had happened over the past month. Actually, I take that back, more like the last twelve years. It was then that the thoughts of my mom surfaced. God, how I missed her. There was so much of my life she missed. I sometimes wonder how it would have been if Carlos had spared her life, and she didn't do what she did so she wouldn't have any children. I wondered if circumstances would have been different for me if she would have just listened to him and stayed with him.

I knew I was thinking selfish thoughts. Had I been in my mom's shoes, I would have done the same thing.

~****~

It seemed as though my eyes just closed when I heard a knocking on my door. "Go away," I yelled, pulling the covers over my head.

When the knocking didn't stop, I knew it was useless for me to try to get some additional sleep; the person at the door wasn't going away anytime soon.

Pushing from the bed, I grabbed my robe from the foot of the bed and went to see who so rudely was keeping me from some much-needed sleep.

Opening the door, Agnes stood before me, holding what looked to be some lightweight sparring gloves and a pair of boxing shoes, which looked to be my size. Wiping the sleep from my eyes and giving Agnes a large yawn, I said in a groggy voice. "Let me guess, Carlos sent you."

"Yes, Miss Nikki. He wants you in the gym in five minutes," she replied

With a roll of my eyes, I took the items from her and closed the door. Just a few more minutes of sleep was all I needed. Setting the items on the end of the bed, I crawled my way to the head and slipped once again under the covers. The bed was still warm, so I found my spot and closed my eyes.

Once again, I heard knocking on the door, only this time it sounded like whoever was pounding on the other side was going to knock the door down. Looking over to the clock, I could see that my few minutes turned into an hour. Jumping from the bed, I quickly changed my clothes and headed to the door. Carlos, who stood on the other side, was ready to kill.

Slipping under his arm, which was propped against the door frame, I looked over my shoulder and said, "Are you coming?"

I knew I should have just got dressed instead of going to bed. The workout with the trainer, who I found out was named Rich, worked me so hard that there wasn't a muscle in my body that didn't hurt. No doubt it was because of Carlos. Taking a seat on the weight bench, I took a drink from my water bottle. Rich was already getting set up for the next phase of my training. As I watched him, he reminded me so much of Sly. Even though he was blonde and blue-eyed, his build was just like Sly's. The way he acted, they could have been brothers. Taking one more drink, I walked over to him to endure one more excruciating workout.

I could barely move when the training finished. His only words were, "See you tomorrow. Soak yourself. It will help," as I stumbled out the door. If he only knew that his training kicked my ass. I'd be lucky if I could get my body up the stairs and into the large tub that he suggested.

Pressing forward, I finally made it up the stairs and into my room. The air smelled like eucalyptus and something else I didn't recognize. As I was trying to undress, Agnes appeared from the bathroom and hurried to my side to help me remove my clothes.

"I don't know why Mr. Giordano needs to be so hard on you," she said softly as she took off one shoe and then the other.

"It's because he's an ass," I replied.

We both looked at each other and then broke out in a laugh. "Don't make me laugh, Agnes. It hurts too much."

"I'm sorry, Miss Nikki, but you are the one who said it," she said with a sympathetic look.

I was really beginning to like Agnes. Even though she had to be at least sixty, she was very kind and her smile was very comforting. I would never be able to understand how someone so kind could work for a man so cruel.

Agnes held onto me as I tried to slip into the tub. The water was so soothing, I could have just slept there and never moved. Extremely content, she tapped me on the shoulder letting me know that she needed me to lean forward in order to wash my back. I hadn't had anyone give me this much care since I was a little girl, when my mom used to give me a bath. Appeasing my curiosity, I asked, "How long have you worked for Carlos?"

She stopped, hesitating before she answered, "Carlos is a very difficult man, even as a boy he was hard to handle. His mother and father were very good, kind, honest people."

Answering my question in a kind of roundabout way, it led to my next question. "What happened to his parents?"

"They were killed when he was a young boy. A drive-by, from what I understand. I didn't start working for him until his uncle requested a nanny for him."

"So you were his nanny?" I asked.

"Yes, since he was six. When he was old enough to take care of himself, he kept me on," she confessed.

"Do you think the death of his mom and dad turned him so cold?" I knew that I was probably being too nosy, but every little bit of information that I could get brought me that much closer to getting out of here.

Finally able to move, I got out of the soapy water and put on more comfortable pajamas, while Agnes turned down the bed. Brushing through my tangled hair, Agnes lightly knocked on the door. Looking at her through the reflection in the mirror, she tipped her head and said, "Your bed is ready. Please don't be late for your training tomorrow. I hate to think about what he might do to you this time."

Nodding at her, I agreed, "I won't."

Watching her leave, it dawned on me that Agnes might be my way out of this place.

CHAPTER TWENTY-THREE

Sly

Peter and the guys had been working with me the past couple of days to figure out a way to get to Nikki. My father, though I hated to admit it, was the biggest help of all. He found out through the grapevine that another fight was scheduled between Nikki and Black Jewel. In a way it was a good thing, because we didn't have to worry about getting past the security at Carlos' estate. There was another obstacle we needed to tackle. The fight was closed to all but the elite crowd, which meant that in order to attend you had to prove you had the funds to pay should you lose your wager.

With these restrictions, it was going to be next to

impossible to get in. The amounts they were talking about were in the hundreds of thousands and there was no way we would be able to come up with that kind of money. Our only choice was to go outside the box and ask for help from Angelo Conti like my father suggested. I knew that if we did that, he would be wanting something in return, and I couldn't let Peter jeopardize Jagged Edge Security's reputation for any amount of money.

"There has to be another way we can get into that fight," I said.

"Well, unless we are invisible, I don't know how that is going to happen, Sly," Peter admitted.

As we sat in the conference room in silence, trying to think of a different way in, Ash slammed his hand down on the table. "Wait, guys, I might have an idea," he chimed in.

Peter and I looked over to Ash, wondering what he had in mind. "You know the place is going to be loaded with security given what happened the last time,"

Ash began, as Peter and I tuned into what he was saying. "Carlos only knows you and Peter, but he doesn't know the rest of the guys. Why can't we be part of the security? All we need to do is figure out a way to get inside."

"There's no way we can get inside posing as security," I replied to his outrageous plan.

"That's where your dad comes in. Angelo, more than anything, wants Nikki to lose this fight. His little scheme to have her arrested didn't work, so if we can convince him that she will throw the fight, just maybe he will agree to allow three of us to act as his bodyguards. I'm sure everyone attending the fight will have their own added security, given the amount of money that will be involved."

"You're fucking crazy, Ash, but you know what, it might just work if we can convince Angelo. The best part is if he agrees, we would be getting Nikki away from Carlos," I mentioned.

~****~

Opening the door to the apartment, I realized how quiet everything was. Over the past week, I had been so worried about how I was going to get Nikki back that it hadn't dawned on me how empty my space really was.

Walking to the kitchen, I pulled a beer from the fridge and began thinking of her. God, how much I missed her. I knew that with the plan Ash had, I needed to have another conversation with my dad. Needing something stronger than a beer, I pulled down a bottle of Southern Comfort and screwed off the lid. I didn't even get a glass. The way I felt, I drank the amber liquid right from the bottle.

Sitting in silence with my bottle of Comfort, I looked out to the city and waited for my father to arrive. I thought that after consuming more than half of the contents of the bottle, I would have felt better, maybe even a little numb, but nothing changed. Instead, I was tenser than ever.

When a knock came at the door, I held up the bottle and downed the rest of the liquid. Setting the empty bottle on the counter, I walked to the door, beginning to feel some of the effects from the whiskey.

The minute I saw my dad, the feeling of sobriety settled in. By the look on his face, I suspected he could tell that I had been drinking. Moving aside to let him in, I blew out a breath in an effort to calm the turbulence that was happening inside my head. I knew that I needed to put my feeling for him aside, at least until Nikki was safely in my arms again.

Taking a seat opposite of where he was sitting, I rubbed my hands over my face, hoping I could clear my mind enough to focus on what needed to be said. "I need your help."

"You know I will help you in any way that I can, son," my father confessed.

After I told him what I needed from him, it didn't surprise me that he was more than willing to help. He even offered to help get Nikki away from Carlos. I didn't know if it had to do with the guilt he had, knowing he was the main cause of my mom's death, or the fact that Nikki wouldn't be with Carlos had he not gone to the police in the first place.

When my dad left, I needed to get it together, My focus was everywhere except where it needed to be. Stripping off my jeans and t-shirt, I needed to clear my head. As I stood under the warm shower, I was drawn back to the many times Nikki and I spent showering together. Just the thought of having her soft body next to mine made my dick so hard it was ready to take off.

Grasping my cock, I began stroking the length, trying the best I could to alleviate the pressure that was building. As the warm water coated my body, I closed my eyes, taking in the warmth, thinking only of Nikki and how amazing the feel of her hands on my body was. Increasing my movements, I imagined Nikki's soft lips wrapped around my shaft, watching her head glide back and forth, working my cock in and out of her sweet mouth. Even though it was my own hand doing the work, it was Nikki I saw kneeling before me, caressing me, sucking and kissing in such a way that there couldn't have been anything sweeter. It had been a long time since I had to jack off, but for me, it was Nikki giving me the pleasure that my body longed for. She was right here with me.

Groaning loudly, I called out her name as my torment took over, spraying the wall with everything I had been holding inside. Placing my hands on the cold tile, I lowered my head and muttered with conviction, "Damn you, Carlos Giordano. Damn you to hell."

~****~

As I laid in bed trying to shut out everything that was tarnishing my mind, I decided to focus on the one thing that mattered. I had only two days to wait. Two days to control my anger and keep my sights on getting Nikki away from Carlos. Someone was right when they said that *'patience is a virtue,'* because right now my patience was just about ready to run out. I had yet to hear from my father and we needed a firm confirmation that Angelo Conti was willing to assist us in our plan. Without him, there was no other way to get inside the fight.

Pouring a cup of caffeine, I looked back to my past, trying to figure out how things got so fucked up. I wasn't a perfect child growing up. Most of my childhood was spent either in the principle's office or on suspension. It wasn't until I was in my teens that my life finally turned around. I knew my future was heading in the wrong direction and if I didn't straighten up, I would be one of those guys that would amount to nothing and end up with a rap sheet a mile long.

I remember for the longest time how much I wanted to be like my dad. I looked up to him for everything, until I found out who he really was and who he worked for. Sometimes I wonder what my life would have been like had I continued to worship him the way I did as a child. I wondered if my life would have consisted of working for the Mob like him. Every day I thank God that I saw the light and chose to do the right thing.

Lost in reminiscing about the past, I didn't hear the knock on the door until I heard my name being called from the other side. Setting my coffee mug down, I quickly slipped on my jeans I had laid over the chair and went to see who was pounding on my door.

I was never so glad to see my father standing on the other side of the door. Giving him a relieved look, I asked, politely, "Can I get you some coffee?"

"Got anything stronger?" he asked as he followed me to the kitchen.

"'Fraid not. I drank the last of my Comfort last night," I confessed.

"Coffee will be fine, then," he replied.

"So, I guess by the look on your face, you don't have good news for me."

"Depends on what you consider good news."

"I'm a big boy. Just let me know what you have." I wasn't sure what my father had to tell me, but good or bad, I needed to know what it was so I could deal with it.

"Angelo accepted your offer, but he wants assurance that Nikki will be throwing the fight. So he has proposed an additional safeguard."

"What kind of safeguard?" I asked.

"He wants you."

"Why would he want me?"

"Think about it, son. If Nikki doesn't follow through with her end of the bargain, then your death will be on her hands," my father explained.

"My death?" I questioned, before I realized what he was getting at. "Are you saying, if Nikki doesn't lose the fight, then he will kill me?"

"That pretty much covers it. I can't let you do it, Sly. I'm not about to hand you over to him. I can't make the same mistake twice."

"It is not your choice to make. And besides, I

know that Nikki will follow through."

"How can you be so sure?" he questioned.

"Trust."

I knew my dad didn't have very much faith that Nikki would lose the fight, but I knew her, and I knew she would do anything to get away from Carlos. I just needed to get word to her somehow of what she needed to do. With the security Carlos had at his estate, it was going to be tough. I already knew she didn't have her phone, and walking up to the door wasn't an option.

The best thing to do was get in touch with Peter. He was the one person who would be able to figure out a way to get to Nikki without raising any flags. Grabbing my leather jacket, I headed out of the apartment and decided to take the scenic route to the shop. Riding my bike always cleared my head, and right now I needed all the clarity I could get. One thing I was crystal clear about was, if I had to risk my life in order to save Nikki's, I would do it for her a million times over.

CHAPTER TWENTY-FOUR

Nikki

"Jesus Christ, Rich, are you on a mission today or what?" I cursed.

"Carlos wants to make sure you're ready tomorrow night. If you lose, he will have my ass."

"I don't know why he's so worried, I got this." As confident as I may have sounded, I wasn't. Being away from training for so long really hurt my stamina. It used to be that I needed to push myself harder because I wasn't getting what I needed from my workouts. Now it was like I could barely get through an hour of anything. It could have been my lack of concentration or the fact that Carlos was calling all the shots. I think it was mostly because I had only one thing on my mind, that being Sly and how much I missed him.

Heading to my room, I was pleasantly greeted by Agnes, who was already preparing my nightly bath with eucalyptus scented bubbles and chamomile. As much as I loved the care she had given me the past week, all I wanted was to be left alone. I only had today before I had to face my destiny. I wasn't very confident that I could win against Black Jewel. Had we fought a month ago, it would have been a different story.

Stripping off my sweaty clothing, I dipped my foot in the bubbly water to check the temperature. Perfect as always. Sliding down into the water, the feel of the hot water was almost as good as an orgasm. Almost, until I began thinking about Sly. Slowly the tears began coming down, adding droplets of water to the already full tub. Sitting in the tub in my saddened state, I was beginning to wonder if I would ever see Sly again. He was the man I was falling in love with and I couldn't even tell him. I might never be able to tell him.

Sinking deeper down in the tub. I leaned my head against the bath pillow that Agnes brought in for me and closed my eyes and pictured the one person that could fill my mind with happiness. I could feel him everywhere, inside me, holding me, caressing my body, kissing me lightly on the cheek and then on the lips.

Lowering my hand, I imagined that it was Sly touching the special place that he could always find. Dipping a finger inside my vagina, I remembered the words he spoke so softly, "God, baby, you feel so good."

It was like he was right here with me, keeping me warm, comforting my soul. With my finger deep inside me, coating it with my wetness, it was only Sly I saw as he began gently gliding his finger in and out and circling my clit with his thumb. Moving my hips to mimic his, every touch was coming from him. Placing my other hand on my breasts, I began caressing them just as though it was Sly kneading them between his fingers. My movements increased as I added another finger, feeling the fullness of his cock as I pictured him in my mind.

I was moving so frantically, needing to escape the thought that this was going to be the closest I would ever come to being with Sly again. Letting my pain take over, it consumed me. The pleasure I wanted to feel turned into an ache my heart would forever hold.

~****~

With the fight less than twelve hours away, I wanted nothing more than for this day to go away. If there was even one possibility of an escape from this hell, I would have taken it in a minute. Pushing from the bed, I headed to the bathroom to do my thing and then face the man who would be expecting me to be ready to train one last time before the big event. I didn't know why I was even bothering with it. I knew I would be no match for the woman I was to fight. I also knew even if I did win, I would lose. If I won I would forever be under the control of Carlos and if I let Black Jewel win, I would be dead the minute I set foot off the mat.

Trying not to think about what was in store for me, I changed into my workout clothes and headed downstairs to the gym. Just as I opened the door, I couldn't have been more happy. I just couldn't understand what she was doing here.

"What the hell….!" I exclaimed excitedly

"Move inside, quickly," Agnes said as she ushered me back inside the room.

I wasn't sure what was going on, but it was a relief seeing Carly. "What are you doing here, Carly?" I asked as Agnes closed the door.

"Your boyfriend and his buddies talked me into coming here. Well, that and they paid me," Carly confessed.

Looking between Carly and Agnes, I still had no clue what was going on. "Agnes, why is Carly here?"

"I am probably going to lose my job over this, but Carlos has done enough damage to you. You shouldn't be fighting, Nikki. You need to be happy, married, raising children. I can't allow Carlos to continue doing these things to you, and when Carly came to the door, I knew she wasn't here because Carlos requested her. She's just lucky that he never answers the door. And when she told me the real reason she was here, I had to let her in," Agnes confessed.

"What's going on, Carly?" I asked.

"Sly wanted me to get a message to you. You have to throw the fight. It's the only way he can assure your safety and get you away from Carlos," she explained.

"I can't throw the fight. If I don't win, he will kill me, not that it matters. Black Jewel will probably win anyway."

"Nonsense," Agnes spat. "You're stronger than you think. I could see it in your eyes when you first came here. I could also see that something inside was tormenting you. I think it's someone that you care about. I've seen it before, when I lost my husband Earl. It's love."

Agnes was right, it was love she saw in my eyes, that mixed with the sadness that I might never be with the one man who could bring me so much happiness. Giving me a quick hug, Carly placed her hand on my cheek and said sternly, "You listen to me, Nikki Jennings. We've known each other for a long time and you will get through this and live happily ever after with Sly. Carlos will only be a bad memory and he won't ever be able to control your life again."

When the two of them left, I waited a few minutes before I headed down to the gym. As I waited, I thought about what Carly said. Maybe she was right, maybe throwing the fight was my way out. Maybe this time, I could finally have my happily ever after.

Rich was already waiting for me with the biggest smile I had ever seen on a guy. I wasn't sure what he was so happy about. This was the worst day of my life. Sitting on the bench, I watched him gather the materials needed to wrap my hands for my workout. As he knelt in front of me, I held out my hand as he expertly began wrapping the adhesive tape around my hand and then in between my fingers, adding a couple of twists. I loved watching him. He did it so well that it was about the only part of my body that didn't ache when the training was over.

"We are going to take it easy today. Carlos doesn't want you tired when the event takes place tonight," Rich explained.

"Well, at least that's a plus," I replied sarcastically.

"He has also instructed me to be there to assist you tonight and to make sure you follow through and win the match."

That was just great. Another man controlling me. It was bad enough having Carlos telling me what to do, now I had Rich to deal with too. Pushing from the bench, I walked over to the speed bag to test out my wrapping and to get in a twenty-minute warm-up. Rich was preparing the exercise ropes in the meantime.

Just when I thought my day couldn't get any worse, Carlos entered the gym wearing his signature black pinstriped suit and a look that could kill. Trying to ignore his presence, I focused on the speed bag.

"I don't know what game you are playing, Nykia, but whatever it is, it isn't going to work," he cautioned.

"I have no idea what you are talking about, Carlos," I hissed.

"I think you do. I found out about your little visitor. Unfortunately for her, her fighting days are over."

"What did you do to her, you bastard?" I cursed, ready to go after him, but before I could, he grabbed my wrist and twisted it behind my back.

"If you don't want the same thing for yourself, I suggest you stop with this silly game. You will never be able to defeat me."

Letting me go, he turned and left the gym just like he entered, with arrogance and malice. He had to be the cruelest man I had ever known. Matter of fact, I wouldn't be surprised if he was Satan's son.

Rich tried everything he could to get my mind off of what Carlos may have done to Carly. I could only imagine what kind of torture he put her through. Halting my punch, my stomach began to tighten. *"What if Carlos found out about Agnes?"* I thought to myself. He would surely kill her. Pulling off my practice gloves, I threw them to the floor and left Rich standing with a confused look on his face. I needed to find Agnes. I had to make sure she was okay.

Jogging to the main house, I opened the front door. Looking around, I wondered where would be the best place to find her. The kitchen seemed like a good place to start. Running through the dining area, I swung open the door, finding that there was no one on the other side. Taking a chance, I ran back to the foyer and up the stairs, hoping to find her in one of the rooms. There were too many of them so I yelled her name. "Agnes, where are you? Agnes?"

When her head popped out of one of the doors, I felt a sigh a relief as she looked over to me with concern. "What is it, Nikki? You look like you lost your best friend."

"Agnes, Carlos got to Carly. He did something bad to her. I thought he got to you too," I cried, giving her a big hug.

"Shh, it's okay, Nikki, Carlos would never hurt me," she declared.

"He's an evil man, Agnes. He would hurt anyone who got in his way. Even you."

I may have over-exaggerated, but Carlos was capable of anything. Sure, he would never do the dirty work himself, but whether it was him or his goons, it didn't matter. As I explained what happened to Carly and what Carlos said, I think that Agnes was finally understanding how afraid I was for her.

"Nikki, as I said before, Carlos would never hurt me. There's something you need to know," she began, leading me to the velvet bench in the hallway. "When Carlos' parents died, there was a safeguard put into place that essentially protected my life, in the event that anything happened to me other than death by natural causes. I am worth more alive than dead to Carlos."

"I don't understand," I said, confused. "How is your safety protected?"

"Without me, Carlos will never have full control over everything his parents left to him, which includes this estate. He would never chance losing it all just to see me dead," Agnes explained.

I had to trust what Agnes was telling me. As much as I didn't trust Carlos, I did trust Agnes.

CHAPTER TWENTY-FIVE

Sly

Everything was set for tonight. I only had another two hours to myself before Angelo's men would be here to pick me up. Peter assured me not to worry, and that Nikki knew what she needed to do. He also promised me that everything would go as planned.

All the guys looked over to me as the bell rang, letting us know that someone just entered the shop. We were all sitting in the conference room. Ash rose to check out who our guest might be. Before he got to the door, my father appeared. With his eyes focused on me, he said in a concerned voice, "Do you have a minute to talk?"

Rising to my feet, I led my father to Peter's office,

where I knew we would have some privacy. I wasn't sure what my father could possibly need to discuss with me, but I had to let him speak.

"What is this about, Gus?" I asked.

"I need to make sure that whatever happens, you stay alive," he confessed.

"So you're telling me this, why?" I asked, waving my hand in confusion

"Because you are the only family I have left, and if anything happened to you, I would never be able to forgive myself. I'm trying to make things right with you, Sylvester. I know I haven't been the greatest father, but I am trying to make up for that. There has been too much hate between us and, well... I just want things good between us."

Maybe my father was being sincere, but there still remained the fact that he chose a life of crime rather than an honest life with me and Mom. I knew that he was trying the best he could to make things right between us, but I didn't know if I would ever be able to allow myself to get close to him again.

"So what is it that you have planned?" I asked, giving him the benefit of listening to what he had to say.

"I'm not saying that Nikki won't follow through on throwing the fight, but in case something happens and she can't, I need to make sure you come out of this alive, so I have included a trusted friend in the mix to make sure that happens."

After my dad explained what would happen in the event something went wrong, I agreed that it was a good plan. Maybe it was time that I began trusting him and mended the relationship that he damaged so badly for such a long time.

My father left after our little talk, not wanting to take the chance of being seen by Angelo's men. I still had an hour to kill, so I headed to the back of the shop, deciding that a little workout would alleviate some of the tension I was carrying. Removing my shirt, I slipped on a pair of boxing gloves and began punching the full length punching bag we had set up in the back of the shop. As I began hitting the bag, the only thought that came to mind was the first time I watched Nikki in action. I think it was then that I realized that she was going to be the only woman for me. The way she concentrated and punched the bag had me hooked. I even remember the little groan that came from inside her as she gave it everything she had, sending the bag spinning.

Hitting the bag hard, I was beginning to feel the tension ease from my body. I wished so badly that I could be there for Nikki, but I knew in order to save her, I had to sacrifice myself.

Concentrating on the bag, I somehow missed the bell ding from the front door. It was only when Ash came to the back of the shop to let me know it was time that I halted my assault on the bag.

If there was ever a time I wanted this to be done, it was now. The smirk Angelo's bodyguard had on his face was about to piss me off. I wanted more than anything to wipe that sarcastic-ass smile off his face.

~****~

The ride to wherever they were taking me was the most painful ride I had ever been on. I felt like I was being kidnapped. The way they had my eyes covered in a black sack and my hands bound behind my back, I suspected they didn't want me to know where they were taking me. Based on the amount of time and the number of turns, I calculated that I was just out of the city. One thing about being in the military, you learned how to calculate where you were in the event you were captured.

The SUV came to a stop and the driver opened his door and got out. Soon he was opening my door and leading me to who knew where. I could feel the gravel beneath my feet, which could mean that we were either in the country somewhere, in the middle of nowhere, or somewhere where there were no paved roads. Taking in a deep breath, I could smell the sea air, so I knew, at the very least, that we were somewhere near the coast.

As they pulled on my arm, the gravel under my feet turned into concrete. I could hear the sound of male voices, but couldn't make out what they were saying. When we stopped for a moment, it had to be so the person leading me could open the door. I didn't have to walk up steps to get inside the building, another clue that I was probably at some sort of beach house.

My senses were focused on everything that was going on around me. Since I couldn't see, I had to rely on my ears and nose to tell me where the hell I might be. And then I heard a voice.

"Keep him restrained until I notify you of the outcome of the fight. I don't want him to get away in case I need to kill him." the voice instructed.

I never met Angelo, but based on the tone of the man's voice, I was ninety-nine percent sure it was him.

Hearing the door open and then close, I was pretty sure I was left with the guy inside. Removing the black sack from my head, I was standing inside a room with no windows. The only thing inside was a metal chair and a television set, which was placed directly in front of the chair. Looking at the man beside me with a confused look, he pushed me down on the chair and said in a deep, arrogant voice. "Mr. Conti wants to make sure you watch what your future will bring."

I should have known that he would have found some way to televise the fight. As the arrogant man secured my hands and feet to the chair, I swore then that the plan my dad had arranged had better work, because if it didn't, I would come back from the grave and haunt him for eternity. Unable to move, I felt more helpless than I had ever felt in my life. I hated not being in control.

Angelo's man stepped over to the TV and turned it on. The picture that appeared on the screen was snowy, which led me to believe that this fight was only being shown to those who had a stake in it. Switching the channels, a fighting ring appeared with a crowd of people sitting around the perimeter. I don't know what Angelo's game was, but as clear as the ring was, he must have wanted me to have a good view of the fight.

Watching the screen with gritted teeth, I could feel my hands grip the arms of the chair with intense rage. The minute Nikki appeared on the screen, my whole body tensed and my anger spun out of control. She looked nervous as hell. Like she knew something that I didn't.

When the other woman appeared that Nikki was supposed to fight, I lowered my head, praying that Nikki would take a fall as soon as the first punch hit her. There was no way she would be able to survive a fight against this he-woman. She had to be twice the size of Nikki, with every inch of her body covered in muscles. More than anything, I was afraid for Nikki and what damage this woman could do to her. I could feel the tension beginning to build once again.

Focusing on the TV, I couldn't hear what was being said, but knew the minute Nikki and the he-woman entered the ring, the fight was close to beginning. A few minutes later a man entered the ring. My guess was that he was the announcer or referee. I watched as Nikki and

Black Jewel walked up to the man. Even with the man's height, Black Jewel towered over him. *How could this fight possibly be even fair?* It didn't surprise me that the odds of Nikki winning this fight were so high. Looking at Nikki and then at Black Jewel, I could tell the man was instructing them in the do's and don'ts of the fight.

When the two of them knocked gloves, Nikki was pushed back by the force of the punch. Whoever this woman was, I had a funny feeling she wasn't going to be playing fair.

Watching Nikki getting the shit knocked out of her wasn't what I wanted to see. I was yelling at her at the top of my voice to take a fall. I knew she couldn't hear me, but I couldn't understand why she would allow Black Jewel to continually pounce on her. When the third round ended and the fourth one began, I thought for sure Nikki would have had enough. The only thing that I could think of was that she wanted to make sure it looked real when she did finally decided to throw the fight.

Just by looking at Nikki, I could tell that she was

in pain. There was a pretty good cut above her right eye and her lip was cut open as well. I could also see a deep red area along her side where Black Jewel continued to punch and kick her. Turning my sights for just a minute, unable to watch the abuse on the TV, I saw Nikki fall to the mat from the corner of my eye. Finally, she was ready to call it quits. When the referee began counting, which I could see as he changed the positions of his fingers through each number, Nikki was beginning to stir, almost like she was trying to stand. Yelling at the screen, I ordered, "Baby, stay down, stay down."

It didn't matter, she couldn't hear me. Somehow I needed to get out of here. As much as I tried to get out of my bindings, it was no use. The harder I pulled, the tighter they got. I felt totally helpless. Unable to help her. To let her know that I was fine and to just stay down. Why didn't the referee call the fight? It was clear to see that Nikki was struggling to get up.

My stomach was in knots as I continued to watch the screen. I couldn't believe how much fight Nikki had in her. Hearing the door open, I turned my focus from the screen to see one of Angelo's cronies entering.

"Looks like your little girlfriend is having a little problem following instructions," he barked.

Without looking at him, I cursed, "Go fuck yourself."

Lifting my chin, he looked at me with disgust before he planted his fist in my gut. I guess he didn't like my suggestion, because no sooner than his fist was in my stomach, his other one followed suit on my face. Looking up at him, I spit the blood that tinged my mouth on the side of the chair.

"I suggest you worry about your little girlfriend following through with Mr Conti's arrangement instead of worrying about who I'm fucking," he said with a chuckle, before he left the room.

I knew the fight was close to being over, or so I thought. Of all the things that were going on, the last thing I expected was for Nikki to go after Black Jewel full force. "What the hell are you doing, Nikki?" I yelled, inside the small room.

Watching Black Jewel stumble, I think she was surprised as much as I was. It was only a matter of time that my life would soon be over. Something changed. There had to be reason why Nikki would be doing this. Someone else must have gotten to her. Changed her mind. *Why?*

CHAPTER TWENTY-SIX
Nikki

Everyone had a choice in life. Mine was to live or die. When I saw Black Jewel enter the arena, I knew that there was no way I would ever be able to beat her. She was at least 5'11' and looked more like a man than a woman. She could have been Grace Jones' sister, except her muscles were bigger and bulging everywhere on her body. Standing there dumbfounded, I was nudged by Rich, who ended up being my coach for this fight. Looking over to him, he could see that I was nervous that this woman would mash me like a hot potato.

"Size isn't everything Nikki. Remember what I taught you," he said with confidence.

I looked over to him thinking, *"Are you serious?"* before turning my focus back to the woman in a man's body. "She's going to kick my ass."

The referee signaled for us to come forward as Rich was making the final adjustments to my wrappings. Standing, I headed to the older man and stood on his left, while Neanderthal woman stood on his right. He checked the adhesive tape on my hands and then my mouth guard first, before he checked hers. This must have been standard procedure for a fight of this magnitude. Usually, only the outside of the gloves were checked for anything sharp or hard that shouldn't be there.

When he finished his inspection, he looked over to Black Jewel and then to me as he recited the rules. "Here's how it is going to be, ladies. No holding your opponent's shorts or gloves. No butting with the head. No biting or spitting. No hair pulling, fish-hooking, or eye gouging of any kind. I want a good, clean fight," he ordered as he looked between us.

Almost losing my balance when we tapped fists, I

walked back to my designated corner where Carlos was standing on the other side of the ring. He didn't look to be very happy. With his index finger, he gestured for me to lower my body to his level. As his lips came to my ear, he began to whisper in a seething breath. My eyes began searching the arena, until she came into view. I would know her anywhere. My eyes began to tear up. I couldn't believe, after all this time, she was actually here.

Hearing the sound of the bell, Rich patted me on the shoulder and moved between the ropes until he was off the mat. Approaching Black Jewel, the first punch took me by surprise. In all the fights I've had, never had a fighter come at me like she did. Feeling a little dazed from the punch, I lost my footing and ended up on the mat. One thing I knew, I needed to protect myself better.

Coming at me again, she landed yet another punch. This time it was to my side, which knocked the breath from my lungs. I wasn't able to back away from her before the heel of her foot landed in the same spot. Every punch and kick she gave landed one right after the other. Sometimes on my face, but mostly on my side.

I needed to get my head into the fight. I was thankful when the round was over. Rich was waiting for me. Unlike the actual rules of legal MMA fights, there are no physicians available to call the fight off. As long as you could still fight, you continued. Another difference was that most MMA fights took place in a cage where the fighters were protected from falling off the mat. I had a funny feeling rules meant nothing to this woman.

As I sat on the small stool, Rich took a look at the cut above my right eye. It wasn't deep enough to cause any concern, but he put some adhesive ointment on it just in case, for added protection.

Round three was worse than round one and two. I actually thought I was going to die. My side hurt so bad that I had a hard time lifting my arm high enough to throw a punch. I knew Black Jewel knew this. She knew the exact place to hit me. Keeping my sore side out of her reach as best I could, she still managed to find a way to get to it. I wasn't sure how much more abuse I could take. When the round ended, I gazed over to Carlos. He opened his suit coat just enough to show me the gun he was carrying. I wasn't sure how he got it past security, unless he had someone on the inside. I knew exactly what it meant. My mind was even more fuzzy and it wasn't just from the numerous punches I got from Black Jewel. I was torn about what was the best thing to do. Either choice would leave someone dead.

Walking to the center of the ring, I had made a hard decision. I only hoped it wasn't the wrong one. With everything I had, I went after Black Jewel with vengeance. She had her fun, now it was my turn. With a left and then a right, I concentrated on the skills I learned, and blocked out the pain that my body had endured. When she stumbled back, I went after her again, only this time it was a kick to her right side. I kept after her, throwing punches, one right after the other, until her skin was a bright shade of red. *'Do unto others,'* my mom used to always say. I say, *"Fuck that."* I wasn't going to let anyone have a piece of me ever again.

Black Jewel either lost her footing or my last punch must have hit her just right, because as I lifted my head, she was on the mat, trying to push herself to her feet. The referee had motioned for me to move back. As I waited for his signal, I watched her slowly rise to her feet. Shaking her head, she set her eyes on me, and boy, was she pissed. I took it that she had never been laid on the mat before.

She was coming at me with full vengeance. I lifted my hands to my chest and waited for her to land the first punch to my already beaten face, only it didn't come. It was like her efforts were in slow motion. Ducking and swinging my body out of her sight, I punched her in the head with everything I had. When she began to wobble on her feet, I twisted around her and planted a punch to the other side of her face. Watching her mouthpiece fall to the mat, my eyes focused on her and I saw something I thought I would never see again. It was the same blank look that Mandy gave me before she fell to the mat.

I took in a deep breath and shouted, "No," as I watched her body fall to the mat. Being pulled by Rich to the other side of the ring, I waited, hoping that I didn't just end the life of another fighter. Putting my gloves over my face and facing the crowd, I heard the referee call the fight. There were cheers coming from the arena, but all I could see was Carlos, smiling as he walked away. Pulling off my gloves, I didn't wait around to be announced the winner. I needed to follow Carlos and find out where he was going.

Jumping off of the four-foot platform, I began working my way through the crowd. Just when I thought I was clear, a strong arm pulled me to the side. Looking over to see who had a grip on my arm, I looked up to hear him say, "We need to get you out of here."

~****~

Ash had such a tight grip on my hand, I guessed it was so that he wouldn't lose me. Pulling on his hand, I got his attention to let him know that I needed for him to stop. "Ash, slow down, I need to tell you something."

Looking at me with concern, he commanded, "Nikki, you can tell me later. You should have thrown the fight."

"I couldn't, Ash," I answered back trying to hold back my tears. "He has my mom."

"What are you talking about, Nikki?" Ash questioned as we continued walking.

"She isn't dead. If I didn't win, he was going to kill her. I had to win," I cried.

"Come on. We will sort all this out later. Right now we need to get you out of here."

I wasn't sure where Ash was taking me, but the only thing I could think about was what a mess everything was. Choosing to save my mom or my freedom shouldn't have been a choice I had to make. Carlos knew exactly what he was doing. He must have found out about why Carly was really at the mansion. He knew all along what I had planned. I just couldn't believe that my mom was still alive. After all this time.

~****~

Pulling up to the shop there were other vehicles parked in front. None of which were Sly's Jeep. My heart fell into my chest. Looking over to Ash, I asked, "Where is Sly? I don't see his Jeep."

"We'll explain when we get inside," Ash replied.

"No!" I demanded. "Tell me now, Ash. Where is he?"

Ash lowered his head, which told me that what he was about to say wasn't good. Looking up at the shop he began, "Angelo Conti made a deal with Jagged Edge. He said he would help us get into the fight with one stipulation. He needed to make sure that he got his end of the bargain, so he took Sly as collateral."

"What do you mean, collateral?" I asked desperately.

"If, for some reason, you didn't lose as planned, then Sly's life would be taken in exchange," Ash choked out.

"Oh God…, what have I done?" I sobbed, placing my head in my hands.

"There was no way you could have known, Nikki. All Sly wanted you to know was your freedom was the exchange. You couldn't have known that Carlos would have pulled his own assurance for you."

"But, Sly could be dead, Ash," I murmured.

"If I know Sly, I'm pretty sure he would have found some kind of back-up plan. He wouldn't have offered his life so freely."

"Then where is he?" I shouted uncontrollably.

"Can we please go inside? Maybe Peter and the rest of the guys have some answers," Ash suggested.

As I got out of the car, all I could think about was Sly. What if something went wrong and he didn't have the chance to put his back-up plan into play? What if

Angelo caught on to his plan just like Carlos did with me? After all, they were of the same bloodline.

When Ash opened the door to the shop, all the guys were there. All of them except Hawk, who was in Kierabali with Isabelle. As I looked around, Brie, who was standing next to her husband Cop, and Lilly, Peter's wife, were even here. I had this awful feeling inside me, just like the day that Carlos showed up at my door, that something was wrong. With my eyes soaked in tears, a little sliver of happiness filled my heart as Romeo came up behind them, running towards me the minute he saw me.

Brie and Lilly walked over to me, each giving me a hug, hoping to comfort me while Romeo, as small as he was, jumped into my arms and began licking my face.. Looking at me, Brie said sternly, "He's okay, Nikki, and don't you dare think otherwise."

I didn't know what to say. I wanted to believe her. And when Lilly looked at me the same way, I knew she was thinking the same thing. While Lilly and Brie were comforting me, Peter's cell began to ring. Breaking our circle, I placed Romeo on the floor and walked over to Peter to find out who was calling.

"Yeah, I understand. Are you sure?" Peter paused. "Let me tell her."

Looking Peter in the eye, I knew something was terribly wrong. It had to be bad by the look on his face. "What is it, Peter?" I asked as Lilly came up beside me, placing her hand in mine.

"It's Sly. He can't be found."

CHAPTER TWENTY-SEVEN

Sly

I wasn't sure what was going on with Nikki, but the minute Black Jewel hit the mat, I knew my life was over. I hadn't heard from my father, and I knew in a matter of minutes Angelo's men would be coming through the door to take care of business.

Staring at the snowy screen, I wondered why no one had come through the door. I didn't know how much time had passed, but I was pretty sure that it had to have been over an hour. Just when I thought maybe my life would be spared, the door opened. Taking in a deep breath, I closed my eyes and prayed that my execution would be as painless as possible.

Feeling the bindings on my hands loosen, I heard

a voice I recognized right away, "We need to hurry," my father said, sawing through the zip-ties that kept my hands bound together.

"It's about fucking time." As pissed as I was, I couldn't have been more happy to see my father than I was at that moment. Freeing my feet, my father pulled a gun from his jacket and handed it over to me. Pulling out the clip, I checked to make sure it was fully loaded. Focusing my eyes on my father, I watched as he carefully turned the knob on the door, and easily began pulling it open. Listening for any movement, he peeked his head out the cracked door to see if anyone was around. Seeing that the coast was clear, he led me down the hall.

When we finally made it outside, two of Angelo's men were leaning up against a black SUV, which I was all too familiar with. Without so much as a word, my father pulled his gun and fired two shots. One hit the taller of the two men in the chest, and the other landed right between the scrawny one's eyes.

It blew my mind how easy it was for my father to

shoot someone without thinking. Helping him drag the limp bodies away from the vehicle, I got in on the passenger side while he took his spot behind the wheel. As soon as we were moving, I looked over to the side mirror for any movement. "Why the hell did you have to shoot those guys?" I said, peering over to him as he surveyed the road judiciously.

"It had to be done. Do you think those guys would have let us live once they spotted us?" he questioned.

My father had a point. I guess I was hoping that there wouldn't be any bloodshed. I had seen enough of it during my time in Iraq. Working for Jagged Edge also had its share of death, even though most of it was in self-defense.

~****~

As we got closer to the city, all I could think about was how much I wanted to wrap my arms around Nikki. I knew that this thing with Carlos and Angelo wasn't over. By now Nikki would be safe and at the shop with the other guys. I couldn't wait to see her. I missed her so much. Just the thought of touching her soft skin, feeling her lips pressed to mine, made me swear that I was never going to let her out of my sight again.

We were within a few miles of the shop when my father pulled the SUV to the side of the road. Placing the vehicle in park, he turned sideways and diverted his attention to me. I wasn't sure what was on his mind, but based on the worried look in his eyes, I knew he had something weighing on him.

"Your mother's death wasn't my fault. You were too young to understand," he began, bowing his head. "She had been sick for some time. I did everything I could for her, even took on an additional job and worked odd jobs on the side when I could. It didn't matter how much I worked, the bills kept coming. Finally, I found a way that we could finally get out from under all the bills."

"So you went to work for Angelo Conti," I contended.

"It was the only way. Anglo took care of everything. The bills, her care. As long as I continued to work for him and do as he asked, she would get the care she needed, only it didn't matter. She died three months later. It was like I sold my soul to the devil."

Listening to my father explain what happened, I somehow felt sorry for him. I knew that something was wrong with Mom. She was always so tired, especially after she got home from her appointments. I never knew where she was, but I remember her always being sick. I could hear her in the bathroom as she spilled her guts. She told me it must have been something she ate. I never questioned her, but when she started losing weight and I would find clumps of her hair in the trash, I knew she had cancer. By that time, Dad was never home and I was left to care for her.

"I knew about the cancer," I admitted as I stared out at the darkness. "I thought you left because you didn't want to deal with it any more."

"That is so far from the truth. I stayed away

mostly because I didn't want to put you and your mom in danger." My father switched his gaze to me. As I looked towards him, I could see the guilt in his eyes as he shook his head in regret. "I hated every minute I was away from her and you. When everything finally blew over, it was too late."

"I hated you for what you did. And when I found out about the Mob, I hated you even more," I confessed. "All I knew was you had chosen a life of crime over us."

"It was the only way, son. I hope that some day you will be able to forgive me."

When my dad finally pulled away from the curb, I finally had a clearer understanding of what happened all those years ago. Sure, he made some really bad choices, but I believe that he was doing the best he could. As sick as my mom was, he didn't cause her death. It was the cancer.

Seeing the shop put a big smile on my face. Even thought there was a lot of shit that still needed to be sorted out, I was happy that I would finally be able to hold Nikki. Swinging open the door, everyone was huddled around her. I wasn't sure that they even heard my dad and me enter the shop.

"Hey, guys, what's going on?" I questioned with concern.

Everyone looked my way with a look of amazement. It was when I saw Nikki that I understood what was going on. Staring right at her, even with her face banged up the way it was, she was still the most gorgeous woman in the room. Pushing everyone aside, she came at me full charge.

She jumped up and wrapped her arms and legs tightly around my body. God, it felt so good to have her in my arms again. As much as I loved her, her grip was so tight that I could barely breathe. "Baby, you need to loosen your grip a little"

"I thought you were dead, Sly. I am never going to let go of you again," she vowed.

"I'm good with that, but could you maybe let go just a little," I whispered as I gave her a gentle kiss on the forehead.

The guys began approaching me, and as much as I hated to, I slowly lowered Nikki to the floor. Peter held out his hand first. "Glad to see you're okay, bro. We were all getting a little worried."

I nodded my head. "I'm sorry, guys, but we may have a bigger problems. Nikki didn't lose the fight." Looking down at Nikki, I could tell she was keeping something from me. "Why didn't you just stay down, baby?"

"I couldn't, Sly," she cried, looking up at me with her beautiful brown eyes. "He had my mom and he was going to kill her if I didn't win. I couldn't let that happen. I didn't know they were going to kill you if I didn't lose.

Her tears began falling uncontrollably. All I wanted to do was pull her closer and try and comfort her. "It's okay, baby. We'll figure this out."

"We need to get my mom away from him. I've lost so much time without her," she admitted.

It would be just like Carlos to pull something so underhanded. I wouldn't be surprised if the woman he claimed to be Nikki's mom wasn't her mom at all. Holding her at arm's length, I gazed into her eyes and asked her, "Nikki, are you sure it was your mom?"

"I saw her, Sly. I know my own mom. Even though it's been a long time since I've seen her, I know it was her."

"We'll get her back, baby. If he has her, we will get her back," I swore. If her mom was still alive and Carlos had her, I would do everything I could to get her away from him.

~****~

Peter dropped us off at my place a little after nine. With all the excitement, Nikki hadn't realized how sore her body was from the beating she took from Black

Jewel. Heading to my bedroom with Romeo close behind, I started a bath for her, hoping that it would make her feel better. My thoughts were somewhere else as I watched the tub fill with water. I knew sooner or later Angelo would find us and finish what he started.

Nikki was standing in the doorway when I finally focused on the water instead of my thoughts. Pushing up from the edge of the tub, I walked over to where she was standing. Cupping her cheeks with my hands, I bent down and kissed her tenderly on the lips. Her lips were still slightly swollen from the emotional roller-coaster she had been on. Lifting her arms above her head, I pulled off her sports bra and threw it to the floor. Her beautifully shaped breasts spilled, causing my cock to pulsate between my legs. Lowering my head, I teased the rosy buds between my fingers while I listened to Nikki's moans of pleasure. Releasing her breasts, I slid my hands down her velvety skin. Hooking my finger in her shorts, I moved them down her legs until she was free of them.

As I admired her body, my cock was protesting beneath my jeans. Lifting Nikki from the floor, I carried her in the tub and carefully lowered her down into the hot water. Removing my own clothes, I slid in behind her. When her butt pressed against my engorged cock, I knew she would be aware of the arousal she was causing me. Pulling her body back against mine, her arms wrapped around my neck, giving me the access I needed to her pert nipples. Her head tilted back further into my chest as I continued caressing her nipples between my fingers.

The hardness of my cock began pulsating between my legs. All I wanted was to be buried deep inside her and feel her warmth wrapped around me. Placing my hands on her hips, I twisted her body so that she could readjust her position. Once she was facing me, I was able to see something in her beautiful brown eyes that I hadn't seen before. "What is it, baby?" I asked as I watched a tear roll down her cheek.

"When I didn't see you at the shop, I got so scared, Sly. Everything in my being just died. I have never felt that way before. I don't ever want to feel that way again. Not with you," she confessed bowing her head.

"Look at me, Nikki." She lifted her head and right then I knew I was totally hers. "I will never leave you, Nikki. I love you more than anything in this world."

Her lips met mine, sending a wave of electricity down my body to the tip of my cock. Even though she has never admitted to me how she really felt, I knew by the way she kissed me that she felt a lot more for me than she was willing to admit. With our lips still connected to one another, I placed my hands on her hips and slowly lowered her onto my shaft. The warmth of her body had me completely undone. It took everything I had not to loss control.

Feeling her walls tighten, I knew that I had touched the one spot where her body would soon let go. I dipped my head slightly and took her mouth with mine. The feel of her soft lips colliding with mine was all I needed to push her over the edge. Her body began to shudder, causing her to take a deep breath. Feeling her breath against my skin, I held her closer. I could no longer hold back my own release. My body gave way to her warmth and my seed spilled inside her. Her center pulsated once more, leaving another round of ecstasy in its wake.

I knew that Nikki was exhausted, Not only by the fight, but also by the burst of pleasure we shared in the tub. Making sure she was tucked away comfortably in bed after giving her two pain relievers, I went to the kitchen to do some soul searching. The last few weeks had been like a hurricane in a shit storm. I needed to take a few and sort things out.

Sitting in my favorite chair, I took a swig of my beer as I looked out over the city of Manhattan. My mind was such a jumbled mess, I didn't know if I was coming or going. First, the confession from my dad and now the possibility that Nikki's mom might still be alive. Oh yeah, and how could I forget the fact that I was a wanted man by the Mob.

Finishing the last of my beer, I knew it was late and the only thing I wanted was to be holding Nikki and focusing my mind on her. Dumping my empty beer bottle in the trash, my phone lit up as it began vibrating on the counter. Picking it up, Peter's number appeared on the screen.

"We have a problem, bro," he said, before I could say anything.

"What's going on, Peter, and do you know what time it is?" I asked.

"Yeah, I know. Sorry, but Nikki may have been right about her mom. Carlos sent over footage from the fight. He wants her back."

"Well, that is never going to fucking happen." Just as the words spilled from my mouth, Nikki appeared.

"What's never going to happen?" she inquired.

CHAPTER TWENTY-EIGHT

Sly

"What isn't going to happen, Sly?" she asked again.

"Nothing, baby. Go back to bed. I'll be right there."

"I'm not going back to bed until you tell me what is going on." There was no way she was going to let this go. She knew whoever was on the phone didn't call at two in the morning to have a friendly conversation. She knew that it had to be important and she would be hounding me until she got the answers she needed.

Keeping my eyes on her, I walk over to the

cabinet and pull down a bottle of Southern Comfort. Grabbing two glasses, I poured one for myself and another for her. Going to her, she gave me an intense look that I knew meant there was a definite problem. Handing her the glass of whiskey, she held it in her hand and just stared at it.

With a deep intake of air, I turned away and said, "Carlos has footage of the fight. He sent it to Peter. He's pretty sure your mom was in it." I turned my body and shifted in a different direction so she wouldn't see my reaction. "He wants you in exchange for your mom's life."

My heart dropped to my stomach as I looked over to her. Just like she said, Carlos knew just how to keep her tied to him. "Then I have to go to him, Sly. If I don't, he'll kill her. He made that perfectly clear during the fight."

"I am not going to allow you to go back to that motherfucker, not after I just got you back. No way, no how, Nikki. End of story. We will find another way."

Placing my glass on the counter, I marched over to her and pulled her body into mine. I always knew exactly what she needed. The last thing that I wanted was for her to be tied to Carlos, but I knew she wanted her mom safe and away from him.

"We will find another way," I reassured her. "Let's go to bed. Tomorrow we will get in touch Peter and figure out a game plan."

Gently lifting her chin, I made sure she saw the sincerity in my eyes. Drawing my lips to hers, I kissed her passionately, letting her know I would not let anything bad happen.

~****~

Peter and the guys were already waiting for us by the time we got to the shop. I knew that with everyone's input we would be able to come up with a way to keep Nikki away from Carlos and get her mom away from him. Nikki seemed to think that Carlos would have taken her mom to his estate. I wasn't so sure that he would do that. While Nikki was being held there, not once had she seen her mom. This made me believe he was keeping her somewhere else.

I hated to think about it, but as close as my dad got to Carlos, he would be the only person that would know where Carlos might be keeping Nikki's mom. So while everyone waited in the conference room, Nikki and I were in Peter's office talking with my dad. When we finished the call, my dad was more than willing to help.

Stepping back into the conference room, the guys were chatting amongst themselves. My guess was that they were trying to come up with a plan. As I took a seat with Nikki resting her tight little ass on my lap, Peter leaned forward to make sure everyone could hear him. Addressing everyone, he began going over the specifics of the plan. His hands were moving with his eyes as he explained what would happen and what everyone's job would be. It would have been an excellent plan, except there was one problem: we didn't know where Carlos was.

"Peter, how are we supposed to implement this plan if we don't even know where the bastard is?" Ash questioned.

Before Peter chimed in on Ash's question, a voice sound from the back of the room. "You guys are wrong. Carlos is playing all of you. I saw him kill Nikki's mom. There is no way she is still alive. If I am wrong, there is only one other place he would take her without drawing too much attention," my father advised.

With the information my dad shared and a plan in hand, we were pretty confident that it would work. Using Nikki as bait was something I didn't agree on. Even though I knew Nikki would be able to handle it and it couldn't be any more dangerous than what she did for Hawk in Kierabali, there was still that chance that something could go wrong.

We all decided it would be best to put the plan into play at night. One thing good about the location where my dad was sure Carlos would be was that he had minimal security there, at least nothing like his security at the estate where Nikki was taken.

Heading out of the shop, Nikki and I got into my Jeep and headed back to my place. It was going to be a short night and we needed all the rest we could get. That was, after we relieved a little tension.

~****~

Nikki and I were supposed to wait at the apartment until we got a call from Peter. My night was shit, even after the explosive sex Nikki and I had. Pacing the floor like it needed to be broken in, I was on edge waiting for Peter's call. Nikki was still sound asleep and I couldn't bring myself to wake her until I knew for sure what they found out.

The plan was that Peter and Ash would check out the residence where my dad thought Carlos would be. If he was there, Peter would call and let us know that the plan was a go. Even though it was still early, I thought for sure I would have heard from him by now. Hearing something stir behind me, I turned around to find that

Romeo was up and ready to be let out to do his business. Once this whole mess was over, Nikki and I would be having a talk about sharing a house together where Romeo could roam freely without being cooped up.

Grabbing his leash and my phone, I opened the door to find two beady eyes staring at me. I knew it was a matter of time before he would show up. As he pushed me back inside, I looked down at the gun he was jabbing in my gut.

"Thought you and your dad could pull one over on me," he cursed as he kept his sights on me while he closed and locked the door.

"You won't get away with this, Angelo," I vowed.

When my phone began to vibrate in my hand, I carefully swiped the screen and pressed speaker. I was surprised that Angelo didn't see it or hear the vibration. Tucking it behind my back when he wasn't looking, I could only hope that the person on the other end wouldn't say anything.

"See, that's the difference between you and I. I'm a lot smarter than you think, and you, my friend, are a lot dumber than you look."

"Here's how I see it, Angelo. If you wanted me dead as badly as you say, I think you would have come after me long before now," I argued, knowing I needed to keep him talking.

Before he could say another word, Romeo really needed to go, so he lifted his leg and before Angelo knew what was going on, peed all over his perfectly tailored suit. Since the gun he had was pointed at me, instead of shooting the dog, he kicked Romeo, sending him crying in the direction of the bedroom.

"First, I'm going to take care of you, then I'm going to take care of that fucking dog," Angelo seethed.

Pointing the gun right at me, I knew my time on this earth was done. It was like everything went in slow motion. The gun went off. I could feel the air of the bullet pass by my ear. *He fucking missed.* When his body began crumpling to the floor, and the blood began spilling from the side of his head, I looked to my left to find Nikki standing there with my gun still pointing towards him. Her hand was shaking and her eyes were focused on nothing but Angelo's body.

Moving toward her, I cupped the hand holding the gun and pulled it out of her grasp. Her eyes were still focused on his body. In a soft voice, she mumbled. "He hurt Romeo."

I almost had to laugh. I knew she was in shock and probably didn't realize that she just saved my life. Pulling her close to me, I kissed her on the forehead and whispered. "I love you, Nikki."

Her eyes finally diverted my way and it finally hit her as to what she just did. Swinging her arms around my neck, she held me like I was the last person on earth. "He could have killed you, Sly," she cried.

"But he didn't. He missed," I assured her.

As she pulled away, there was a long streak of blood on her arm. Placing my hand to my ear, I rubbed it lightly to find that he did manage to graze my ear. Nikki's eyes filled with concern as she inspected the damage. When she took in a sigh of relief, I knew it wasn't so bad.

It was then that I remembered that my phone was still on speaker. Pulling it from behind my back, I looked down at the screen and said, "Peter?"

"What the hell is going on over there?" he asked, unaware of what just happened.

"A problem that needed to be taken care of," I responded. "You might want to call in a favor to the NYPD."

By the time I filled Peter in on what happened and the NYPD were notified, Jagged Edge Security would be receiving a commendation for getting one of the deadliest Mob leaders off the street. It didn't help with the situation with Carlos, but at least there was one less thug to worry about.

As we left the condo, I could tell that Nikki was still in shock from shooting Angelo. Even though she pretended to be fine, I knew she wasn't. I was ready to call the whole thing off and suggest that we find a different way to get to Carlos. Nikki wouldn't have it, though. She wanted, more than anything, to see the look on Carlos' face when his empire began to crumble.

It was getting close to dark and we had gone over the plan at least a dozen and a half times since the initial plan changed. Carlos contacted Peter to let him know where he wanted to meet. Peter was a pretty good judge of character and he knew that Carlos wasn't falling for us just handing Nikki over so freely. We needed to be prepared for anything and everything. That's why we decided that Peter and I would meet Carlos for the exchange, while Ash, Cop, and Lou headed to Carlos' home to rescue Nikki's mom. We were pretty sure that his security would be minimal since his greatest threat would be the exchange.

~****~

Nikki was on pins and needles as we sat in the Jeep waiting for Carlos to arrive. Placing my hand over hers, her eyes met mine. "It will be okay, Nikki. You know what to do?' I asked, watching her nod her head up and down.

"When I walk over to him, I'll pretend that I stumbled and twisted my ankle. While he's attending to me, Peter will be behind him, placing the small explosives on the back tires. Once I see that it has been done, I'll stand and proceed to walk to the vehicle, keeping up my act and limping as I walk towards it."

"Good girl," I said, smiling at her. "The explosives should go off within two minutes of the vehicle moving. Do you have your watch on?"

I wanted to make certain that Nikki knew how long she had before the tires would explode so she could be prepared herself should the driver lose control of the car. The speed shouldn't be excessive so she should be able to get out without any injuries.

Lifting her wrist, she showed me her watch and smiled. I knew she was nervous, but if everything went as planned, her mother would be safe and Carlos would be either dead or spending the rest of his life behind bars.

As I gave her a kiss, a black SUV came into view, letting us know it was time. We waited for it to come to a full stop before exiting the car. When the SUV stopped, Nikki and I got out of the Jeep. Just as we closed the doors, Carlos and one other man stepped out of the SUV. One thing we didn't count on was them carrying weapons. Reaching for mine, I was halted immediately.

"Not so fast, Capelli. Throw your weapon down or Nikki dies along with you right here," Carlos cursed.

I had no other choice but to throw down my weapon. "We're here, Carlos. No need for weapons," I yelled towards him.

Carlos began to laugh. "You think I am going to believe you are just going to hand Nikki over? How dumb do you think I am? Kick your weapon over to me."

Taking a step forward, I kicked the gun in his direction. I watched as it slid across the pavement, stopping short of hitting his foot.

"Okay, now you, Nikki," Carlos demanded.

Looking over to Nikki, I gave her a reassuring nod and watched as she began walking over to Carlos. Counting to five in my head, I waited for her to fall. Just like clockwork, she pretended to twist her ankle and stumble to the ground.

"Ouch, holy crap," she cried.

I watched as Carlos' man walked up to where Nikki had fallen. Even though Carlos didn't move from his spot like we had thought, he was still so focused on what was going on with Nikki that he didn't notice Peter putting the explosives in place.

"Enough," Carlos shouted. "Pick her up and let's get out of here."

Just as his sidekick was ready to lift her from the pavement, Nikki cursed, "Get your slimy hands off of me. I can walk."

I was doing a high five in my head. I had to hand it to her, she was definitely made for this line of work. Not that I would ever admit that to her. Pushing herself from the pavement, she began hobbling over to the SUV where Carlos was waiting by the door already open for her.

I waited until the SUV was out of sight before I got Peter and made a U-turn in the same direction that they were headed. Looking at my watch, I figured that there was about a minute and a half left before the explosives went off. Staying far enough behind the SUV, Peter and I began counting down the seconds when Peter's phone rang.

"Hewitt," Peter answered.

Looking at his expression, I could tell something was wrong. Ending the call, Peter slammed his hands against the steering wheel. "What's going on Peter?" I asked concerned.

"Ash and Cop got to Giordano's house. Turns out Nikki's mom was none other than a look-a-like that Carlos had been fucking for years. I guess he really was obsessed with Nikki's mom."

Within a second, the mini bomb went off and the back end of the SUV lifted from the ground. Just as we suspected, the driver lost control of the SUV. The one thing we didn't take into consideration was the possibility of the driver ending up in the water. Pressing my foot on the brake as hard as I could, I held on to the steering wheel as the Jeep skidded to a stop. Watching the Escalade take flight, it hit the water and began sinking, fast.

As Peter and I ran as fast as we could toward the sinking SUV, we watched it go completely under. Removing my boots while still running, I wanted to be prepared to dive into the cold water. Reaching the edge of the pier, I dove in as Peter called the police.

The water was like ice as it hit my body. Getting my bearings, I surfaced long enough to take in a couple of deep breaths so I could fill my lungs with air. Going under, the water was so murky that I had a hard time seeing anything, and with the SUV being black, it was even harder. Looking around, I noticed a few air bubbles in the distance. Swimming over, I could see the vehicle more clearly. I knew I was on the wrong side of the SUV when I spotted Carlos' dead body through the window. Swimming over the top, I placed my hand along the top so that I didn't lose track of where I was.

Looking in the window, I could see Nikki pounding on the glass. I tried to open the door, but the pressure of the water made it impossible to move. There was a little air space inside the SUV, but it was filling up fast. Signaling her to move back. I found the weakest part of the window and began thrusting my elbow against the glass.

It was no use, I needed something stronger to break the glass. I was running out of air too. Swimming to the surface, I once again took in a couple of deep breaths to fill my lungs. Diving back under, I noticed that the back window of the SUV was already cracked. It must have happened when the bombs went off.

Holding onto the frame, I used the heel of my foot and kicked the glass free. Within seconds the SUV filled with water, taking away any air that may have been left. Pulling the on the broken window, it finally came loose and floated away. Reaching inside, I grabbed anything I could to pull my body inside.

When I got to Nikki, she was still buckled in. I tried to free her, but the latch wouldn't budge. Pulling a knife from my pocket, I began cutting the strap. I don't know where the extra strength came from, but I pulled the strap until it finally tore completely apart. Pulling Nikki free, I got her out of the SUV as fast as I could, I knew she couldn't hold her breath much longer, and my air was running out as well.

We finally reached the surface. All I could see were red and blue lights. I held on to Nikki as I swam to shore. The rescue team was already lowering a ladder into the water. My body was so exhausted that I could barely move, but I knew I needed to push on. When a hand reached for me, I knew we were safe.

CHAPTER TWENTY-NINE

Nikki

"Sly, Romeo needs to be let out and I did it the last time," I yelled, pulling the covers over my head to block out the light that was coming through the window.

"Yeah, yeah, I heard you," he yelled back as he walked up to the bed. "You know we could take care of this problem."

"We are not getting rid of Romeo. He is the only family we will ever have."

"I wasn't talking about that, baby, I was talking

about moving. I could sell this place and we could buy a house. Something outside of the city where Romeo could run. Maybe we could even get him a playmate."

"You would really do that? Sell all this?" I asked, waving my hand in the air in a circular motion.

"Yeah, why not?" he responded with a smile.

Throwing a pillow in his direction, I playfully said, "Take the dog out."

Getting out of bed, I knew it was going to be impossible to go back to sleep. As soon as Sly got back with Romeo, he would be on the bed wanting to play. That was how it was every morning.

As I turned the water on in the shower, I thought about what Sly said. Maybe it was time to get our own place. With his income and my new job at Jagged Edge, we would be able to find a pretty nice home. A home I knew we could never fill with children, but we could have lots of animals.

Hearing the front door close, I didn't realize I had been in the shower that long. Turning off the water, I grabbed my towel and began drying myself. Wrapping my wet hair in a towel, I headed to the bedroom to get dressed. Romeo was already laying on the bed making himself at home in the spot I just vacated. Walking over to him, I gave him a little pet before I began getting dressed.

I could hear Sly out in the kitchen, probably cooking one of his famous dishes. Out of everything I loved about this man, his cooking was one of them. Pulling my t-shirt over my head, I walked out to the kitchen to find my man slaving away at the stove. Giving him a small loving pat on the ass, I reached above my head and pulled out two coffee mugs.

Sipping my coffee, I watched as he expertly flipped over the eggs without breaking the yolk. Something I was never able to master. With a smile, he kissed me on my forehead and turned his body, placing one egg on my plate and two on his.

Taking a bite of the wonderful meal, I got lost in my thoughts, thinking back to when Sly and I first met, how much we had been through over the past month. I guess there is a reason why things happen. I guess I needed to stop over-thinking things. Even though Sly knows how much I care about him, I still haven't shared the 'L' word with him.

Grabbing my plate, I walked over to the sink and rinsed it off before placing it in the dishwasher. Just as I was about to finish getting ready for the day, Sly came up behind me and gave me a sweet kiss on my neck. His kiss was so tender that it sent a wave of electricity from the tip of my tongue to my core. There was always something about his touch that always had me undone. Pulling him closer to me, I deepened the kiss as our tongues mingled together, tasting the essence of each other.

Sly moved his hands down my body, sending a tingle to my core. Placing his hands on my butt, he took it in his grasp and lifted me closer to him. My arms tightened around his broad shoulders, locking our bodies closer together. Lifting me from the floor, I could feel his hardness as it pressed against me. The thought of what was to come heightened my arousal, leaving a rush of pleasure through my veins.

Heading in the direction of the bedroom, our lips once again reclaimed each others. The kiss was soft, yet persuasive, as my lips parted for him. Sly couldn't have settled me on the bed quick enough. My hands were on his clothing, ripping and tugging it savagely, until it was completely off.

Breaking our kiss, his eyes were on me, devouring every inch of my clothed body. Leaning over me, he said in a hushed voice that turned my senses inside out, "I think you have way too many clothes on." Lifting my t-shirt over my head, my breasts fell free, full of life as my nipples were erect and awaiting his touch. Watching him intently, his eyes were focused on my exposed breasts. I could see the satisfaction in his stare as he lowered his head and captured my taut nipple between his lips. Swirling his tongue, a tingle of excitement radiated down my body. With a gentle tug, he took my nipple between his teeth while placing circular movement with his tongue. My back rose from the bed as heat rushed between my legs.

Slowly Sly moved down my body, kissing every inch of my sensitized skin. With a sweet whisper, he gazed up at me saying, "I love these," as he moved back to my breasts, kissing and licking my hard peak. "And I love this," moving his mouth to my stomach. "I really love this," he claimed, dipping his tongue inside my navel. "But of everything, I mostly love this," he breathed, placing his tongue over my clit. Just his words alone sent my body skyrocketing. Before I could feel him inside me, my orgasm took flight, coating my folds.

Sly's mouth moved lower, lapping up the juices my body offered him so freely. Lifting his head, he looked up to me with glistening lips and said with contentment. "I love you, baby."

Turning my head to the side, my heart swelled with warmth, because I knew that I loved him too. While I bit down on my lip to keep my sobs at bay, Sly moved his body up mine, filling me with his fiery brand. Everything inside me broke. It was then that I knew there was truth to my feelings. I loved him more than anything in this world. Screaming his name, my floodgates broke and my secret was revealed.

"What is it, Nikki? Did I hurt you?" he asked in desperation.

"No," I said silently, unable to speak.

"What is it? What did I do?"

"You loved me," I confessed. "You showed me what it feels like to be loved."

"I have always loved you."

"I love you too, Sly." I cried, looking deeply into his soul.

"I will never get tired of hearing you say that," he said, brushing the tears from my cheek. "Say it again, baby."

"I love you, Sly Capelli."

"I love you too, Nikki Jennings." he replied before lowering his mouth to mine and kissing me with a tenderness so soft that it sent another spiral of ecstasy down my body.

"So I guess that's a 'yes' on the house."

We looked at each other and began to laugh. There was nothing more that I wanted than to spend the rest of my life with this man. Knowing my mom was really dead, Sly was my family now. He not only saved me, he loved me too.

A.L. Long

About the Author

My passion for writing began a little over two years ago when I retired from a nine to five job. Even though I enjoyed working, I wanted something different. It was then that I decided that I wanted to write. Romance and passion is a topic that everyone desires in life, and it is for that reason I decided to write Erotic romances. Finding my niche as a romance writer has not only filled my heart, but also has kept me young. When I'm not writing, I like to spend time outside taking long walks and sipping wine under the stars.

I hope you found **SLY** enjoyable to read. Please consider taking the time to share your thoughts and leave a review on the on-line bookstore. It would make the difference in helping another reader decide to read this and my upcoming books in the Jagged Edge Series.

To get up–to-date information on when the next Jagged Edge Series will be released click on the following link http://allong6.wix.com/allongbooks and add your information to my mailing list. There is also something extra for you when you join.

A.L. Long

Coming Soon!!!!!!

Ash: Jagged Edge Series #5

Read all the books in the Jagged Edge Series

Hewitt: Jagged Edge Series #1

Cop: Jagged Edge Series #2

Hawk: Jagged Edge Series #3

Sly: Jagged Edge Series #4

Other books by A.L. Long

Next to Never: Shattered Innocence Trilogy

Next to Always: Shattered Innocence Trilogy, Book Two

Next to Forever: Shattered Innocence Trilogy, Book Three

To keep up with all the latest releases:

Twitter:

http://twitter.com/allong1963

Facebook:

http://www.facebook.com/ALLongbooks

Official Website:

http://www.allongbooks.com

A.L. Long

49676988R00226

Made in the USA
San Bernardino, CA
01 June 2017